smart
CASUAL

E MCGREGOR

Contents

For Gunny, the 'Social hand grenade',

Much missed.

CHAPTER ONE
Mistake

Davie Wilson would go anywhere for football, or more specifically, he would go anywhere for football violence. If he was being honest, going to watch the actual games didn't interest him anymore. Against Modern Football and all that shite. He had been going with Rangers ICF firm since the late 1980's when he was just a teenager and had travelled (and fought) the length and breadth of Britain. He'd been on countless eventful European trips, and he'd still kept going looking for trouble when Rangers had been demoted through the leagues, even though the likelihood of a row was virtually non-existent.

In the early days Davie and a few ICF had gone with Partick Thistle and their NGE firm. He still knew a few Thistle lads. However, they had the same problem's which affected most firms nowadays: not enough active numbers, not enough decent games and far too much police attention when there actually was a decent game. Plus, the cunts were pally with Aberdeen these days.

Davie had been with a few other Scottish clubs over the years as well and with some Rangers to Chelsea which were great trips to see old friends. Once, he had also gone with a few of the younger lot to Germany for a Hamburg game, but the German's have got it all wrong. Stone cold sober seven-foot bears with gum shields and UFC gloves doing press ups and fighting in a forest with fucking cameramen and medics on hand ain't the one.

Davie had friends or contacts at most of the Scottish firms and loads of English ones. Over the years since the action had dried up, he'd started 'guesting' with a few of these mobs if they had a promising fixture on the horizon. It was far from ideal, but beggars most certainly couldn't be choosers these days. Today,

Davie was going to be a guest of his friend Paul Wood from Hamilton. Hamilton are, and always have been, a proper shit mob but they had some good lads in years gone by, it's just a pity they were let down by the rest of them. The Hamilton mob or ACF (Davie had no idea what it meant, no one else seemed to know or care either) were piss poor. However, Woody was a mate and he'd phoned Davie earlier in the week and said there was a good chance of it going off against Airdrie. He'd asked him if he'd fancied coming along and before Davie knew it, he'd agreed. It was the League Cup and Airdrie had been on the phone saying they would have a mob out. Airdrie may be a shit football team and an even shittier place to live but one thing they seemed to take pride in was their firm, the Section B. Davie had been part of Rangers mobs in the past which had run amok against Airdrie but going with Hamilton was a different matter altogether.

Davie knew Hamilton would get done but that made it all the more fun. There was nothing like being outnumbered and still giving it a good go. Some people thought he'd lost the plot with this attitude, or his brain wasn't wired up properly, but Davie loved it. If he had his way, he'd take a small, tight firm of good lads everywhere with Rangers, but the good old days had ended, and he was reduced to this. Going with fucking Hamilton Accies. He hadn't told any Rangers that he was planning on going. They'd rightly try and talk him out of it. Plus, let's be honest, he wasn't going to shout it from the rooftops that he was joining the elite Hamilton Accies casuals for the day now, was he?

Davie met Woody as he got off the train at Hamilton West train station and walked with him to meet the rest of the Accies mob.

'How many you got out today mate?' Davie asked.

'Hopefully have a good 30 or 40.' Woody said. He was wearing red and white gazelles, and a fucking daft looking red Stone Island jumper which had seen better days. It was as if he wanted to be a casual and a bloody scarfer at the same time with this get up.

The two of them entered The Hamilton Vaults pub. It was only a minute's walk away from the train station and quite frankly a fucking ridiculous place to have a mob meeting up. Especially when the chances of it going off were as high as Woody claimed they were. The police would clock them all in here but maybe that was the idea. Easier to say they'd been wrapped up by old bill than to admit they couldn't match Airdrie.

If Davie was disappointed at the venue, he was absolutely raging when he saw the rag tag mob gathered in front of him. Even Woody had the good grace to look a little sheepish. There were around 20 lads, and the term 'lads' is used very loosely. Half of them didn't look old enough to be served at the bar and the older ones didn't look like they'd be able to fight their way out of a paper bag. Davie knew right away that this was a big mistake. Airdrie would go through this lot like a hot knife through butter. For fuck's sake, even Clyde would go through this lot.

'You up for this today big man?' A little Hamilton runt decked out from head to toe in fake Burberry check asked Davie after he'd been introduced.

'Is this it?' Davie replied, again surveying the twenty or so bodies in the pub. He knew he shouldn't be anywhere near this. He should be using his return train ticket and getting the fuck out of there. However, Davie's decision-making process was always letting him down.

'Should be a few more out mate, but this will be enough. It's all about quality not quantity.' the wee fanny laughed before wiping coke from his big greasy, spotty beak. He had obviously never seen quality before if he thought this was it.

At around 2pm Woody got a call. Airdrie had arrived. Everyone finished up their drinks. Davie may have been surrounded by one of the worst mobs ever assembled in the entire history of football violence, but he still had a good buzz at the knowledge that it was going to go off any moment now. The younger Hamilton lot looked full of bravado which was probably due to the amount of coke they'd sniffed. At least they looked up for it.

By this stage there were around 25 Hamilton. They all left the pub together to meet their fate. They turned the corner and immediately spotted a mob of Airdrie further up the road. There were around 40 Section B which pleasantly surprised Davie, he'd thought they'd be well outnumbered, but 40 against 25 wasn't too bad in anyone's book. He'd take they odds any day of the week. The Airdrie lads started running down the road towards them. No police in sight. Maybe this wasn't a mistake after all. Fucking come on!

Davie had to resist the urge to shout ICF. He stepped forward, bouncing on his toes, ready for the incoming surge from Airdrie.

That's when he felt it. Something was wrong. Airdrie were slowing down. Davie looked to his left and then to his right. No one was beside him. He turned around and looked behind him. They'd all legged it. Every single fucking last one of them. Even Woody. He should have trusted his instincts; it had been madness thinking that any other outcome was possible. Deep down he knew this would happen, yet still he had followed through with it.

4

Airdrie had nearly reached Davie now. They'd pulled up short. There was no way they were going to catch the Hamilton shitebags. Even the older lot had run away like fuckin Linford Christie at the height of his steroid use. They were nowhere to be seen.

'The fuckin cunt's left me.' Davie said to no one in particular. Airdrie's mob were pishing themselves with laughter. This was like a red rag to a bull, if there was one thing Davie hated more than anything else in the world it was being laughed at.

'C'mon then, let's fucking do this.' Davie shouted at Airdrie's mob, some of which had already started to depart, disappointed that Hamilton hadn't stuck around for a fight.

The smaller number of Airdrie who were left looked at each other and then at Davie, not really knowing whether to take the liberty being offered to them.

'Give it a rest mate, eh? Away and join the runners.' An older Airdrie lad said, chuckling away to himself. He was beyond scruffy, he looked like something straight out of the early eighties, with his skinhead, ugly green bomber jacket and fuckin maroon Doc Martens.

'Who the fuck you laughing at ya fuckin tramp?' Davie, unwisely, said.

'Fuck it, c'mon then ya daft bastard.' The trampy Airdrie lad shouted. Davie flew into the group, connected with one decent punch before he was overwhelmed by sheer numbers. Punches and kicks rained down on him. He fought as best he could, but then he went down, curled into the foetal position, and tried to cover his head. Just before he blacked out, he heard someone say:

'The daft cunts had enough.'

CHAPTER TWO
Spitting games

'Look at the state of your face!' Laura Wilson was furious.

Davie had phoned ahead to try and warn his wife that he'd been in a bit of a 'scuffle' and had a few cuts and bruises, but it most certainly hadn't done the trick. Laura wasn't daft. She knew Davie still ran about at the football, but she was assured that nothing happened anymore and on the main, Davie was telling her the truth. Laura wasn't buying his story that it had nothing to do with football and had been a random attack outside the pub. He'd tried to tell her that Rangers weren't even playing. Yet, somehow, she was still unhappy and of course it was all his fault, as per fucking usual.

'How are you going to go to work on Monday with your face looking like that?' Laura asked. Flecks of spit landed on Davie's cheek. This always seemed to happen when Laura was angry, she'd lose control of her saliva. As for work on Monday? He hadn't thought that far ahead. Davie was more a live for the weekend type of guy. Laura always had been the thinker in the relationship.

'I'm due some time off, plus I can work in the office for a bit, means I'll avoid going out to people's homes. It'll be fine. It's not as bad as it looks anyway.' He had to admit, it did look bad, and it stung like a bastard. However, Davie had to try and reassure her. This would all blow over.

'For God's sake, you've got all the answers, eh?' Laura said. Davie could feel a fucking speech coming on here. She didn't seem in the least bit concerned that he could've been seriously injured. All she wanted to do was shout and spit at him.

'Olivia's parent's evenings on bloody Tuesday and Allan's is next week. If the bruises aren't gone by then there's no chance you're coming with me!' Laura spat, 'No way am I explaining to their teachers that my husband's a big stupid wean who gets into fights at the football. You're forty-seven years old for God's sake. Forty-seven! In three years, you'll be fifty!" Laura was laying it on a bit thick here, Davie thought. Plus, his face was soaking. In three years, he'll be fifty? Nobody needed to be hearing that, especially after just having the shite kicked out of you by the fucking Section B.

Davie's face was still stinging like fuck, and Laura's ranting and raving wasn't helping matters one little bit. It wasn't just his face either, the fuckers must've done some damage to his back and ribs as well, he was in agony. The only good news to come out of this whole shitfest was that he'd avoid Olivia's and possibly even Allan's parents evening at the school. Every cloud and all that.

Davie now knew that he should've gone to the pub and gotten blind drunk instead of coming home early to face Laura's spittle. It was always easier listening to his wife arguing with herself when he'd had a skinful. He should have gone anywhere else but home. If truth be told, Davie knew he really should have gone to A & E, but he was fucked if he was waiting about there for hours on a Saturday afternoon.

Some of the looks he'd been given on the way home as well, people looking at him as if he was the scum of the earth just because he'd obviously been in a fight. Did it not cross these people's minds that he could have been the innocent victim of an unprovoked attack? People were always far too quick to judge.

Davie made his way past Laura, her spitting and her moaning and headed to the fridge for a much-needed cold beer. He also grabbed a few painkillers from the kitchen cabinet and washed them down. For good measure, he took a large bag of frozen peas from the freezer and made a show of applying them to his swollen face. He'd known Laura would've been angry but what could he do? He'd come home with all sorts of injuries and tall tales before, and it hadn't been the end of the world, so what was different this time. She'd get over it. She always did.

'How are the kids?' Davie asked, trying to change the subject. He was glad that they both seemed to be out. Allan wouldn't have minded but it would have upset Olivia seeing her dad like this. Laura obviously wasn't wanting to move the conversation on, she scowled at Davie before stomping from the room without saying another word. She made her way upstairs. Melodramatically thumping on every step as she went.

'Can you fling us down a towel?' Davie shouted up after her, knowing this annoyed the fuck right out of her. 'My face is soaking from all your spitting.' Nothing, no reply. The silent treatment. Yet he was supposed to be the 'big stupid wean'. This suited Davie just fine. He heard doors slamming up the stair with a fair bit of force behind it. She could be a right fuckin drama queen at times.

Davie found the remote control and clicked the television on. Then he put his feet up on the couch and tried to forget about the piss poor day he'd had so far.

CHAPTER THREE
Shoot the runner

After the kicking he had taken, Davie vowed to himself that he would never go with such a piss poor mob like Hamilton ever again. It was bad enough getting done when he was running with his own firm Rangers, on the odd occasion it had actually happened. And don't let anyone kid you, every firm has been done at some point, but being done when you were with a mob like Hamilton? It was fucking embarrassing. He had to knock it on the head. He would knock it on the head. Davie knew that if the Airdrie lads hadn't stopped when they had, he could've ended up a hell of a lot worse. It was another lesson learned the hard way.

His so-called friend, Woody, had eventually plucked up the courage and texted him late last Saturday night asking if he was alright and to apologise. He said it shouldn't have happened and he'd got caught up in the numbers running. Davie, as yet, still couldn't bring himself to compose a reply and Woody, wisely, hadn't pressed the matter with any follow up messages or phone calls.

Davie was meeting up with a few Rangers lads for a beer as he did most Saturday afternoons. Good company, a few pints, a gram of gear and hopefully a wee win on the coupon. In the absence of any potential football violence, it was the next best thing. Plus, it was always good to bring out the old war stories with like-minded people.

'What the fuck happened to you Wilson?' Scott McKee said as Davie entered the pub. The swelling and bruises had reduced but his face was still a bit of a multi-coloured mess, plus he was limping a little bit and kept holding his bruised ribs. His choice to wear a cap to the pub as some sort of disguise hadn't helped as much as he thought it would.

Davie was embarrassed to even tell his story but knew he would have to offer it up at some point. There was no use in delaying it or trying to brush it off. Some of the younger lads knew what had happened already and had been in touch through the week but so far, they'd kept their mouths shut. With the internet these days, nothing could be kept secret. Every detail (normally including photos and videos) was posted on Facebook or WhatsApp or fuck knows where else within two minutes of the event. Basically, they were always making the Old Bill's job much easier than it should have been. Police nowadays didn't have to do much digging to find out what had happened at the football. They were being presented with all the information they needed to make a few arrests. Scott McKee wasn't the type to go searching on social media to find out about any offs though, he was old school and Davie wasn't sure the guy even knew how to work a computer or a smart phone.

'I stupidly went to Hamilton v Airdrie with Paul Wood last Saturday and they gave me a going over.' Davie said. The truth would come out sooner or later. There was nothing to be gained from making up some cock and bull story, only to get caught out in a lie later.

'Daft cunt.' McKee said. 'You need to stop going with tin pot mobs like that mate.'

Davie didn't need to be told. 'I know mate.'

'It'll give us a bad name if it ever gets out that a Rangers lad is running with shite like that.'

Davie hadn't really considered this, but he supposed McKee had a good point. It made sense. He wouldn't be back in any case. He'd learned his lesson.

'Dae Celtic no go with Hamilton?' Billy McKay piped up.

'Not that I know of.' Davie said.

'I heard they all ran like fuck, is that true Davie?' Young Andy Paton said. He was smirking. Paton knew fine well it was true as they'd discussed it numerous times through the week on the phone.

'What?' McKee said. 'They all left you to take a kicking?'

'Yeah mate.' Davie said.

'That's fuckin shocking.' Andy Paton said, still smiling. 'Bang out of order.'

'What about your mate Woody?' Billy McKay said, he had met Woody a couple of times before and hadn't really taken to him.

'He was on his toes as well.' Davie admitted. Billy looked as if he was taking Woody's sprinting personally.

'Fucking hell.' Billy said, shaking his head before gulping down the remains of his pint.

'I know. But what can you do? I live and learn.' Davie tried to laugh it off as best he could.

'You can smash utter fuck out of them. That's what you can do.' McKee said, slamming his bottle down with anger. A few other drinkers in the pub looked over but soon turned back to their own conversations when they saw the look on McKee's face.

'Aye, find out where they drink, and we'll take a mob down. We'll fucking smash them.' Billy added. He had perked right up at the thought of future violence.

Davie hadn't really thought about the situation like that, but the lads had made some valid arguments. Why should he let it go? Woody had invited him to join them and then he and the rest of his mob had taken flight and left him to rot. What was he meant to do, just put it all down to experience?

Davie knew he had been daft to go along in the first place, it was a recipe for disaster. Airdrie were always going to run over the top of a mob like that but there was no way he should just let it go. Cunts like that deserved some comeback. Shitebag's like that gave casuals a bad name.

'You's up for it?' Davie said. 'I know exactly where they drink.'

'Too right mate.' McKee said, with a manic grin on his face. 'Let's get it organised.'

'I'm sure Celtic used to go with Hamilton.' Billy said to himself.

Davie's mind was now doing overtime. Things had just gotten very interesting indeed. Hamilton and that twat Woody wouldn't know what had hit them. For the first time in days, he started smiling. Davie was brought out of his daydream by the lads bursting into laughter. It took him a moment to realise that some

13

clever fucker at the jukebox had put on 'Shoot the Runner' by Kasabian. Davie couldn't help but join in with the laughter.

One thing was sure though, revenge would be fucking sweet.

CHAPTER FOUR
House of Horrors

Davie had been a financial advisor for around twenty years now. He'd started off working for a company but had been self-employed for the past five years now, which was far more to his liking. Davie never had been good at being told what to do. He dealt with all sorts of weird and wonderful financial queries although if he was honest, it wasn't the most exciting job in the world. Part of his job required him to go out to customers' homes and try to get them a good deal on buying a new house or on re-mortgaging their current property. He would also help folk with pensions, or any other money matters they had. He couldn't complain as he made a reasonable enough living, and it wasn't the hardest job on earth.

Davie was good at the job and normally made sure his customer's got the best deal possible when it came to financial products. Of course, he took a commission on the services he provided, he had to make money as well, otherwise what was the fucking point? Normally, he tried to keep his personal feelings about a person out of the equation but sometimes it was just not possible. Sometimes it could not be avoided. Today was one of those occasions. He was visiting a house in the Maryhill area of the city, not too far from Partick Thistle's Firhill stadium which brought back fond memories. However, this was no ordinary house. He'd received a call from a young woman who wanted him to come out and meet her father who was planning on re-mortgaging or potentially selling the property. The woman had sounded pleasant and polite enough on the phone but when he knocked on the door, he immediately regretted taking the call and arranging the house visit.

A woman with hardly any teeth opened the door and flashed him a gumsy grin. She was dog rough and wearing a Celtic top. This wasn't a rare occurrence. There was no avoiding it in a city like Glasgow. However, this woman had the full kit on; shorts and socks the lot. She was one step away from wearing football boots and shin guards. As he entered the property, Davie knew that this wasn't going to be like any normal house visit he'd ever had before. The whole house, every last fucking inch of the place, was covered in Celtic colours and memorabilia. Celtic flags, Irish flags, a big photo of the Pope, a huge Celtic clock, photos of Jock Stein, Tommy Burns, and other notable Celtic pricks lined the walls. The walls themselves had been haphazardly painted in green and white hoops. Or at least that had been the initial idea. It looked like they'd got bored halfway through. There was also a big fuck off green rug taking up most of the living room floor. The place was absolutely fucking horrific. Davie felt his stomach turn over, he felt physically sick. How could anyone live like this?

The Celtic clad woman with no teeth led Davie into the living room, showing off the number 67 on her back with 'The Big One' emblazoned above it. Davie was too shocked at the whole scenario to laugh. He was introduced to her elderly father who was sat on an old chair covered with a green throw. He too was resplendent in the Celtic home top although this one seemed to be three or four sizes too big for him and a couple of years out of date. His also had a multitude of stains all over it. Low and behold he had hardly any gnashers either. Davie tried his hardest to remain composed. There was a little girl running about as well, he presumed Naeteeth's daughter, she was wearing a Celtic onesie. Of course she fucking was. What the hell was going on in here? Davie wouldn't be surprised if Jeremy Beadle popped out at some point. Maybe one of his mates was at the wind up and this was all being filmed for the telly.

'What happened to you then?' the gumsy daughter said, upon noticing the now fading bruises on Davie's face. His face had turned a lovely mix of blue, purple, and yellow.

None of your fucking business ya gumsy cow was what Davie wanted to say but he opted for 'I was in a small car crash, nothing to worry about.'

'WHERE THERE'S BLAME, THERE'S A CLAIM!' the old father shouted far too loudly and then proceeded to have a right good chuckle to himself. The old guy was so loud Davie had nearly shat himself.

'Da, you're shouting again.' NaeTeeth said to her father who was still laughing away at himself.

'My dad's a bit deaf, you'll need to talk quite loudly for him to hear you but I'm here to do the listening for him.' She smiled again, flashing her tooth. Naeteeth was taking advantage of her father, Davie thought. Plus, the old guy wasn't that deaf, he'd heard Davie when he said he'd been in an accident. She was probably making the senile old cunt re-mortgage or sell the place to give her a wedge for new dentures.

Davie endeavoured to try and get out the house as quickly as he possibly could. He would get them any deal which was available, no matter the rates. Anything to let him leave unscathed. He had started to sweat and was having horrible visions going through his mind as the woman spoke for her father: this is where he would die, killed by a family with no teeth and Celtic tops galore. No one even knew where he was, he'd not told anyone where he was going today. They'd chop him up in little bits and bury him out in the green gazebo which he could see out the back. Davie hadn't heard one word the woman with no teeth had said. He stared blankly at her.

'Are ye no going tae write any of this doon?' she said.

'I normally get my clients to email me their situation, means I don't miss anything. Plus, it'll be better that way due to your father's hearing.'

'WHAT DID YE SAY?' old faither piped up. 'THE HEATING'S BEEN FIXED!' Davie shuddered at the volume.

'Well whit was the point in ye coming here then?' NaeTeeth said. 'I cleaned the place up and everything.'

Fuck knows why I'm here love, but if I was to hazard a guess, I'd say that someone up there is well and truly fucking testing me, Davie thought. Plus, if this was her cleaning the place up, he'd hate to see it on a normal day or after a heavy weekend.

'YOU WANT ME TAE TURN THE HEATING ON? PROVE TO YE IT'S FIXED!' Old Faither bellowed.

'Can you help us oot with the hoose or no? My da needs this done as soon as-' NaeTeeth continued. She was desperate to get her hands on the old man's readies. She was almost pleading.

'GET ME SOME GINGER, EH?' The old dad shouted, cutting his conniving daughter off.

'In a minute Dad, this is important.'

'I can help you out, don't worry. I'll email you with some options.' Davie said. 'What's your email address?'

'It's kellycmonthehooops@gmail.com but hoops has three o's.' Gumsy said as if it all made absolute perfect sense.

Davie wasn't even going to ask; he scribbled the ridiculous email down.

'WHERE'S MA FUCKIN JUICE?' Old Faither shouted, he stamped his feet on the floor for good measure this time. Davie sensed the old guy was going to launch into one any second now.

'Dad, in a bloody minute.' His loving daughter said.

'Right, I'd better be off, I think you'd better see to your dad. I'll be in touch.' Davie said, eagerly trying to edge towards the door.

'JUICE!! WHERE'S MA JUICE?!'

'Aye, well can you email me quick about it, this needs to happen soon, I- my dad can't be worrying anymore about it.'

'I'll email you as soon as possible, thanks for your time.' Davie was just about at the front door now. He could almost taste the fresh air. The freedom.

'Aye, be sure and do that.'

'Here's my card, my numbers and email are on it-' Davie had blurted this out before he could stop himself, he reluctantly handed over his business card. You daft bastard, Davie thought, why the fuck did you give her the card.

As the door was being closed and Davie was breathing in the fresh air, he could hear the old guy shout 'HAIL! HAIL!' at the top of his lungs as if it was the most normal thing in the world.

CHAPTER FIVE
Military operation

Rangers were playing Livingston at Ibrox. It didn't get much more glamourous than that. Davie and eight of the ICF were in the pub early but there was absolutely zero chance of a row. After all, it was fucking Livingston they were playing. Livingston were lucky if they'd bring fifty fans, never mind anything resembling a mob. In Davie's opinion, teams like Livingston were everything that was wrong with modern Scottish football: hardly any fans, terrible lifeless stadium with a plastic pitch, no mob and they brought a fuckin drum with them everywhere they went.

Rangers would roll over Livingston and win by at least two or three, but Davie had decided he wasn't going anywhere near the ground today. If truth be told, he didn't enjoy going to the games anymore. Football was ruined nowadays. Herded about and filmed by old bill. Paying 30-40 quid (or more) for a ticket to watch substandard pish. Matches played at fuckin 12:15 on a Sunday with limited numbers of away fans. All these dicks with smart phones filming the entire game and blogging about it on YouTube. In the good old days, these pricks would have received a well-deserved dart in the fuckin head.

Years ago, everyone went everywhere and more often than not, it kicked off. No matter who you were playing. Bring back the fuckin 80's. Or even the 90's. The younger ICF lads had heard all the old stories about numerous offs in years gone by until they probably thought they were there themselves. There was no doubt about it: CCTV, the internet and mobile phones had fucked it all up. Turning a corner and bumping into forty or fifty other likeminded lads in some shithole like Montrose and it going right off was nearly a weekly occurrence. And it was very rare that anyone got the jail. Even if they did, it was normally a slap on the wrist or a poxy fine. Just about everyone had a mob as well. Davie had been involved in brilliant fights with some ridiculous teams in some weird and wonderful locations. Teams that had bizarre mob names as well. The chookter cunts at Montrose called themselves the Portland Bill Seaside Squad for fuck's sake. Teams that had absolutely nothing nowadays had firms years ago and it was class. Davie remembered one time going to St Johnstone at the old Muirton Park and it went off before, during and after the game. Same at places such as Dunfermline, Ayr and even at fuckin Arbroath. They days were magic. Davie got a feeling sometimes that the younger ones thought they were making half the stories up. Nowadays, there was no point in going to places like Perth. It was either:

a) A lifeless all seater stadium in the middle of nowhere with no hope whatsoever of a fight. Or,

b) a shit town with shit pubs and being followed about by Football Intelligence officers with absolutely no hope of a fight.

Not to mention that most of the time the games were probably moved for the telly to 12pm on a Sunday.

In saying that, Rangers always had some sort of mob at every game they played and if it was being offered by any opposing firm, they were more than willing to take part but the whole scene was fucked now. A good number of ICF lads had been jailed for fighting against Wigan in pre-season a while back. Some nosey bastard had posted videos online and made the old bills job far too easy for them. The social media clips were everywhere, then the news sites picked them up. This highlighted the risks associated with still going looking for trouble. It was fuckin terrible the way football lads were treated. The sentences dished out were mental. The other week Davie and Laura had watched a documentary about poor little Sarah Payne. She was murdered by a scumbag

21

paedo who'd been in jail for abducting and tampering with another little girl. The beast went to jail in 1995 and fuckin came out again to abduct and kill Sarah Payne in 1997. Unbelievable. It made him sick hearing that. Davie knew guys that had been jailed for years for fights with other football lads and then when they came out it was tags and banning orders and signing in at local police stations every other day, yet these fucking nonces could walk about scot free to offend again and again, it was fuckin scandalous.

'What you doing here anyway Wilson?' Billy McKay said, snapping Davie out of his daydreaming.

'What you on about?' Davie said.

'Thought you'd be away mobbing up with fucking Stranraer or some shite looking for a row.'

Davie supposed he deserved a bit of a slagging after what had gone on. In fairness, his friends had gone quite easy on him.

'You had any thoughts about when we're going to smash these Hamilton fannies?' Scott McKee said. He was bouncing around the table, the guy rarely sat still.

'I have as it happens.' Davie said. 'They play St Mirren at home, a week on Friday. Live on the telly for fuck's sake. They'll be out for that.'

'You know where they'll be before the game?' Andy Paton said.

'Aye, pub right beside the train station.' Davie said, 'The Hamilton Vault's or something like that. That's the boozer they use. Terrible place for a mob to meet up but that's where they'll be.'

'Show us it.' Paton said.

'How can he show you it, ya mug?' McKee said.

'Google maps' Paton said. McKee had never used Google maps in his life, he struggled with his ancient old Nokia, probably still played snake on it.

Davie told young Paton where the pub was located and thirty seconds later, they were huddled around looking at an aerial shot and the surrounding areas on his phone.

'Fuck me it's like a military operation.' McKay said, coming back with the drinks.

'Operation Shoot the runner.' Andy laughed.

'Operation Kasabian.' Davie said.

'Aye, very good, let's stop fucking about and get down to the serious business.' McKee said, not seeing the funny side.

'How will we get through?' Billy said.

'We could get the train-' Paton started.

'No.' McKee said, cutting the youngster off before he'd even got started. 'We'll use the minibus. Train leaves it wide open to being spotted. Get the minibus in, park as close to the boozer as possible. That side street there should be fine.' He pointed it out on the phone. 'In and out with no fuss. Catch everyone unawares. We'll be on the motorway back here before the Old Bill know anything's happened.'

Even Paton had to admit that this sounded like a much better plan. This wasn't going to be a normal day out at the football after all.

'We'll need to think about making some plans for the final as well lads.' McKee said.

If Rangers beat Kilmarnock, then they'd meet either Celtic or Aberdeen in the League cup final next month at Hampden.

'We're no even there yet. Knowing our luck, we'll probably bottle it to fuckin Killie.' Davie said.

'Nae chance. Don't be talking all that negative shite around me. We'll be in the final, no doubt about it. We'd better be prepared, you know what they say: fail to prepare and prepare to fail, or some shite like that.' McKee said. A few people laughed but immediately stopped when they saw McKee wasn't joking one little bit.

CHAPTER SIX
Parent's evening

Davie had been dragged along with Laura to his son Allan's parents evening at his Secondary school. He'd missed Olivia's the previous week due to the bruising on his face as apparently Laura was too embarrassed to take him. Davie wasn't too bothered about missing out. He'd have preferred not to go to Allan's either if he was being honest. Allan was in third year at school and was a reasonably smart kid. He got involved in a bit of bother now and again, but who didn't?

Rangers were playing at Hampden in the League cup semi-final against Kilmarnock and if they won tonight, it was Celtic in the final after they had pumped Aberdeen in the other tie. He hoped that once he'd left the school after a tortuous night speaking to teachers that he'd be greeted by some good news of Rangers progress. That ought to be the case anyway, but you never knew. Stranger things had happened.

Davie hadn't thought long or hard about what to wear to the school, so he was a little taken aback when Laura was horrified at his choice of outfit. The yellow Stone Island jacket was an absolute belter and one he would never wear to the football in case he got caught on CCTV doing something he shouldn't. 'Yes, your honour the guy was wearing a bright yellow SI jacket ...' Laura didn't think it was appropriate for the school parent's evening, but Davie was fucked if he was going to leave it in the car, it was Baltic outside, plus somebody might try the motor for it. He had at least agreed when Laura had told him to 'lose the bloody cap'. He had acted like the adult in the relationship, compromised and left it in the glove compartment.

Davie and his wife were waiting to see the English teacher when something, or rather someone, caught his eye. You can always feel it when someone is staring at you, it's like a sixth sense. Davie turned to the side to see a man boring his eyes right into him. The guy was wearing a suit and tie but didn't look like a teacher. His suit was trying but failing to cover up his haggard face which carried a few nicks and scars. He wasn't going to be advertising skincare products anytime soon. Maybe he was admiring the nice yellow jacket or maybe-

'Mr and Mrs Wilson, if you'd like to come over?' The English teacher, a tiny old woman in her sixties or seventies called over.

Davie and Laura proceeded over to the old teacher but the guy in the suit still eyeballed him as he moved. What's this dickhead's problem? Davie thought, thankfully not out loud. Maybe he'd helped him get a mortgage? It must have been a right shitty interest rate he'd been given because the haggard cunt didn't look happy at all.

'Good evening, Mr and Mrs Wilson, thanks for waiting.' the tiny, shrivelled woman said. She looked even older up close; Davie had never seen so many wrinkles before. Laura was saying a few words, but Davie's mind was elsewhere.

Was this guy Celtic? He looked like a guy who used to jump about with them years ago, a little balder now but then again who wasn't? What the fuck would he be at this school for if he was Celtic though? Maybe he was Thistle? He was pally with a few of them but there were always folk who didn't like you because you were Rangers. It's just the way it was. Davie was more than used to it.

'Allan is doing very well. He's come on leaps and bounds since last year. A little distracted sometimes...' The wrinkled pensioner was wittering on and still the guy with the hacket face was growling at Davie. What the fuck was this Celtic prick looking at? Davie's phone buzzed in his pocket; someone must have scored in the game.

'Here's the marks Allan achieved for...' Davie looked over the piece of paper thrust in front of him and nodded as if in agreement, but he wasn't really taking any of it in. He glanced over again at the starey prick with the bad skin and received a kick on the leg from Laura for his troubles. She must have noticed he wasn't paying one bit of attention to the elderly teacher's gibberish.

'Any questions you'd like to ask?' Mrs Benjamin Button asked.

'No, no, thanks very much.' Laura said, thankfully bringing the meeting to a close. Davie hadn't heard much of what was said if he was being honest.

As they were leaving, Wrinkles called over to the other's waiting.

'Mr and Mrs O'Shea, if you'd like to join me?'

O'Shea? He fuckin well was Celtic. Fuckin Tony O'Shea. That's who it was. Davie knew he recognised him. Pockmarked faced prick. What the fuck was his son doing at this school?

'What's going on with you tonight?' Laura said. She looked annoyed but she was trying to keep a lid on it because she was in a school surrounded by teachers and other parents. She couldn't shout and spit here without making a big scene.

'Nothing's going on.' Davie said, 'I'm fine.'

'Well, stop acting so bloody weird.'

Even at a school's parent's evening, football violence was at the forefront of Davie's mind. If he could lose Laura, he could wait for the Celtic knobend outside. Ask him who the fuck he was growling at. O'Shea had always been a game fucker, but he'd taken numerous kicking's from the ICF over the years and maybe he wasn't wired up properly anymore. Tony fuckin O'Shea. Would you believe it. The ugly bastard had written a book years ago about Celtic's exploits all over Europe, pity it was made up of half-truths and outright lies. Exploits over Europe, don't make me fuckin laugh. Punchbags of Scotland more like, never mind Europe. As if anyone would want to read about fuckin Celtic and their piss poor mob.

'You're not listening to a word I'm saying, are you?' Laura looked mad. He hadn't a clue what she'd just said.

'Stop you're moaning. Let's get this over with, who's next on the list?'

'Mr Hetherington, Maths.'

Laura moved on. She walked with real anger in each quick step. Davie held back; he quickly checked the message on his phone:

'Rangers two up at half time - easy mate'.

Davie smiled at the good news, put the phone away and made sure to make a wee detour before the next teacher meeting. So what if Laura got even angrier. He walked back over to Tony O'Shea, leaned down until he was close enough to be heard.

'Hope your kid's as good at fiction as his old man.' Davie whispered into O'Shea's ear. He walked on smiling to himself. O'Shea sat stone faced. Raging. His pockmarked face twitching.

Sometimes in life it's the small victories that count.

CHAPTER SEVEN
Man to man chat

Laura had told Davie he was to have a word with Allan about some of his behaviour at school. Davie was a little surprised at this as he'd thought his son's school report had been quite decent compared to previous years. However, in fairness, he had to admit he'd missed some of the things the teachers had said. Well, most of the things they'd said. It was that Celtic twat O'Shea's fault. How was he meant to concentrate with him roaming about the place growling? He should've left his phone at home as well; it had buzzed every two minutes with updates on the game at Hampden and possible plans for the final. Who schedules a school parent's evening the night of a cup semi-final anyway? Inconsiderate bastards.

Davie and Laura had argued all the way home in the car afterwards, something to do with Davie not paying attention to anything important and being easily distracted. Laura was so angry, the windscreen looked as if it'd been raining from the inside. Now, Laura was expecting him to have a man-to-man chat with Allan so fuck it, that's exactly what he was going to do.

Davie knocked on his son's door which seemed to be permanently closed. He heard some music playing. He knocked a bit louder and then there was the sound of a lock being released. Davie didn't know there was a lock on the door. The wee man must've put it on himself because Davie certainly hadn't. Which was a little bit worrying. Eventually, the door creaked open, and the smell of his son's room smacked him around the chops. Davie almost staggered backwards. What the fuck was the boy doing in there?

Thank fuck I'm not young anymore, Davie thought as he heard the noise which was passing for music playing in his son's room. Some of the absolute pish that youngsters listened to these days. Davie had tried to get Allan into The Stone Roses, The Charlatans, even a bit of Oasis but what was Allan listening to? Stormzy. Fucking Stormzy! And before any of you start it had nothing to do with the colour of his skin. Davie had never been like that. He'd happily stand with anyone, as long as they were sound enough or game enough. Racism wasn't the one for him. Back in the day loads of football lads had got caught up in all that right-wing Combat 18 nonsense but Davie had stayed well clear.

Davie wasn't even against rap music, it's just Stormzy, for fuck's sake. Davie had told his son numerous times that if he wanted to listen to some proper rap then he should get himself some Public Enemy on the go. At least they were decent. He'd seen them live a few years ago when they'd supported The Prodigy at the SECC although, if he was being honest, that night was a bit of a blur after someone had spiked his pint with all sorts of Mandy.

'Turn that shit down, eh?' Davie said as he entered his boy's room, cleared a pile of clothes off a chair and took a seat.

'It's stinking in here pal, want to open the window a bit, let some fresh air in?' Davie said. It wasn't stinking. That was being kind. Very kind. It was absolutely fucking reeking in the room. Allan turned the music down a touch and then slowly walked over and opened the window an inch. He didn't look best pleased at the intrusion into his smelly lair.

'What is it?' Allan said.

'Your mum wants me to have a word-'

31

'Tell her everything is fine.' Allan said, cutting his dad off. Davie laughed. This was going to be hard work.

'Is everything fine?' Davie said.

'Aye, brand new.' Allan said, he wasn't even looking in Davie's direction. His son was a right wee huffy cunt at the best of times, but he looked right pissed off at this whole scenario.

'You know you can talk to me about anything son, if anything's bothering you.'

'Aye, alright Dad.'

'I mean it pal, if anything's bothering you just give me a shout.'

Davie knew he wasn't going to get much out of Allan about schoolwork or life in general, so he decided to press him on other matters.

'Is there a boy called O'Shea in your year?' Davie asked, if he didn't want to talk about school there was no way of forcing him.

'Yeah, Charlie O'Shea, we call him Big Chas.'

Fuckin Big Chas. Don't make me laugh.

'What's he like?'

'Aye, he's alright, a quiet big guy.'

'Is he a Celtic fan then?' Davie asked.

'Aye, I guess so but he's not into it the way you are.' Allan said. Davie had been caught unawares with that answer. What did he mean by that?

'A couple of older guys in the school go with the ICF, well there in the Union Bears but they go with the hooligans or so they say.' he continued.

'Oh aye, what's their names?' Davie said.

'Grant McPhee and John McCallum.'

Fuck, Davie knew them. Grant McPhee especially. They were in the pub quite a bit. Had been involved in a few scuffles. Davie had taken a few lines from Grant. That was embarrassing. Running about with school weans. They were sound enough lads right enough, but Davie hadn't realised how young they were. Didn't know they were still at bloody school. To be fair, Davie and loads of his mates had been running about with the ICF since they were teens, so it wasn't a huge shock that it still went on today. Running about with his son's pals though, sniffing gear with his son's pals, there was something not right about that.

'If mum asks, can you tell her I gave you a good talking to son?' Davie said. 'You can't be bothered hearing it and I can't be bothered saying it, so let's just tell her we had a right good chat. Tell her I got angry, started shouting at you and threatened to burn all your Stormzy CD's or something. Tell her you're going to buck up your ideas or some shite like that. She'd appreciate it.'

'No bother Dad.' Allan said. Davie could see that his son wanted him out of there and Davie wasn't keen to stay much longer. What the fuck was that smell?

'Oh, and spray some air freshener or something in here pal, it's fucking howling.'

CHAPTER EIGHT
Cup final day

A lot of time and effort goes into trying to organise a row at the football these days. Especially one that would be as well policed as a national cup final at Hampden between two old rivals. Unfortunately, the days when you simply turned up at a game or a town centre and there were opposing mobs waiting on you around every corner were long gone, never to return. There were no mobile phones and no social media to get in contact with opposing mobs back then, but it still seemed to go off every other weekend. The police were different back then as well, they weren't clued up at all and just wanted to pack you back on the train and get you the fuck out of their city. Nowadays, they are itching to jail you for even minor things. They seem to take casuals presence in their town or city personally. They film you, take your photograph and jot down your details every time there's even the slightest chance of trouble and still when there's no hint of bother. Davie had lost count of the number of Section 60's he'd had.

Davie had been for a few beers with some of the top ICF lads over the past couple of weeks to finalise plans for the Cup final. Celtic had been in touch with a few of them and said they'd have a mob out. Celtic said a lot of things mind you but surely to fuck they'd be right up for it on cup final day against their hated (but rated) rivals.

Everyone was buzzing about the final, but Davie wasn't too bothered about the actual game. Of course he wanted to see his team win, especially as it was against Celtic but if he was being honest, he was much more interested in getting a result off the park. He didn't even have a ticket for the game which would have been unheard of years ago. He hadn't even tried to get one. Rangers had been in that many cup finals over the years, Davie couldn't remember how many he'd been at. Maybe if it had been a European final he'd want to go, but then again, he hadn't got a ticket for the finals in Manchester or Seville, and it hadn't been the end of the world. They'd both been great days.

The anticipation of the day arriving meant that Davie had hardly slept the previous night but if he was being honest, it was nothing to do with the game itself. It was the thought of meeting up with his pals and hunting down the CSC that had made him rise at an ungodly hour.

For the first time in what felt like years, just about everyone was out for the occasion. Faces Davie hadn't seen for ages. However, it wasn't some sort of old school reunion, this was serious business. Celtic had been bumping their gums to some of the lads that they'd have a huge mob out, but many Rangers would only believe it when they saw them with their own eyes. Davie thought to himself that there must be a fucking republican march on or something because that's the only time these cunts could pull half decent numbers and they still ended up getting done or turning up with an escort. In saying that, Celtic's firm seemed to have amalgamated with that Green Brigade lot these days so maybe they would have numbers. Maybe they'd dress all in black with balaclava's then try (and fail) to attack a pub full of pensioners again.

Celtic would need a big mob to have a go at Rangers today. In fact, scratch that, they'd need a fucking miracle to have a go at Rangers today and not get well and truly turned over. Rangers must have had nearly 200 lads out which was no mean feat these days. Considering the old bill had been going around some of the lad's doors and workplaces during the week telling them to stay away from the fixture or risk being arrested, a mob of around 200 was impressive. The hassle football lads received from the police was unreal and Davie could fully understand why a lot of lads had more or less given the whole thing up, everyone had a lot to lose. Giving up wasn't in his makeup though. He never had been a quitter.

Every Rangers lad hated Celtic and their poxy firm with a passion. It wasn't just Rangers, most lads from all the different firms around Britain hated Celtic with a passion. It wasn't any Catholic/Protestant religious nonsense, although that did go on of course. Some on both sides of the divide were obsessed with that stuff. It wasn't that they'd had results against Rangers or any other firm for that matter either. Davie had lost count of the number of times the ICF had smashed Celtic everywhere. It was just that, well... it was fuckin Celtic. Everything about them was just fucking wrong.

Rangers mob were in three different pubs not too far away from each other. In the pub Davie was in, they had bunged the landlord a few quid so as they could get into the lounge which was separate from the main bar in the hope that this would evade any old bill who stumbled across them. It was catch 22: have the full firm in the same pub (if they could find one big enough to accommodate them) and then if the OB came across them that would be it. Or, split the mob up and have them spread over different pubs which made the chances of at least one mob going undetected much higher. They'd decided on the latter plan, splitting everyone up into different boozers and Davie was praying that it wasn't his lot that picked up the escort.

The pub was different on the day of a big game like this, especially when there was a good chance of violence. Everything seemed more tense, and everyone seemed to be more focussed. Most lads were drinking and sniffing, but the vast majority weren't drinking and taking gear as they normally would. You needed your wits about you on a day like this. There were obviously those who couldn't help themselves and ended up in a bit of a state, but if it came on top then Davie didn't want to be too steaming and not do himself or the mob justice. The kick-off for the final was at four. Davie had left the house at ten and his mob had been in the boozer since opening time. So far, they had remained undetected. There had been phone calls back and forth between the two mobs, supposedly Celtic had a good firm out, but if that was the case then why were they saying to have it after the game? The plan had been to try and have a meet just before kick-off, but Celtic had said they fancied it later. Giving firms the run-around as usual. Some of the younger lot were out and about trying to spot any Celtic, to see if attacking their boozer was a viable option but, as yet, they hadn't come across them. It was like a big game of fucking hide and seek. The day was turning into one of frustration and it was imminently about to get a lot worse.

'Celtic's mobs on snapchat.' Young Grant McPhee announced.

'What do you mean they're on snapchat?' Billy McKay said.

'There's a video of them walking about, posted five minutes ago.'

Right enough, the wee guy from Allan's school wasn't lying, Celtic were on snapchat and the videos were now being shared in WhatsApp groups Davie was in. The scene really was fucked nowadays. Snapchat for fuck's sake. Why feel the need to post videos of your mob walking about when there was a good chance of trouble in the air? Why feel the need to post incriminating videos where you can clearly make out lads faces? Bring back the 80's and 90's with no phones or fucking social media. No wonder football violence was dying out.

'Where abouts are they? Can you tell from that video?' Davie said, sensing an opportunity to hunt down the CSC.

A good few lads were now checking their phones to see if they could garner any more information or watch the video which had been posted. The clip showed a group of Celtic walking, you couldn't tell where they were but at least they were out.

'Aw shite, there's another video, it's on a guy I know's Snapchat. Celtic have been picked up by the old bill already.' Big Evans said.

'You're fucking joking.' Billy said.

'There not the only ones.' Davie said, looking out the pub lounge's window.

'Aww fuck right off!' McKee shouted before slamming his bottle down hard on the table. All around conversations stopped. Everyone wondered what had happened and then it became crystal clear. It was the dreaded moment when you looked out the window and saw the meat wagons lined up outside.

All the planning was for nothing, and the game was well and truly a fuckin bogey.

CHAPTER NINE
Fucking Football Intelligence

The Football Intelligence walked into the pub's lounge and had a look around. Two of them, although there were many more normal uniformed Old Bill positioned outside. The two FI officers looked ridiculously chuffed with themselves. Rangers main football copper was the big lanky cunt who currently looked like the cat who'd got the cream and then some. He was called Peter Gilmour but most of the lads called him 'Happy' which he didn't like one little bit, so 'Happy' it was. He tried to dress like one of the lads but failed miserably as most polis do. He stuck out like a sore thumb. He was with a smaller Football Intelligence fanny who Davie thought was called Mikey. He didn't particularly care about his name. All he cared about was the fact that this odd couple seemed to be taking great pleasure in shutting down any fun which could have taken place.

The two Football Intelligence were looking around the boozer, mentally taking notes on how many lads were in the pub and seeing how many they knew. They were having a wee chuckle to themselves. If they were even half decent at their jobs, they'd realise that this was only a third of the mob but most of these guys didn't have a clue. Most of them were bullied at school and had a huge chip on their shoulder as a result. Thought they were the bee's knees at dinner parties because they traipsed about after big bad football hooligans all day and wore a bit of Stone Island. Thought they were a ticket because they talked to casuals and knew them by name. Complete and utter arseholes, every single last fucking one of them.

At around half three the Rangers lads with tickets started to make their way to the ground whilst Davie and the others without tickets stayed put in the pub, much to the annoyance of the coppers. The lads who had tickets for the game were escorted to Hampden by dozens of old bill, on foot, in vans, dog units, the whole fucking shebang. The remainder who were left were stuck in pubs getting followed and harassed every minute of their day. The day was a complete washout. They had tried to leave the pub they were in by phoning taxis, and it had worked for all of ten seconds before the plod had clocked what was going on. Everyone then had their details taken and had been filmed even though nothing untoward or illegal had actually taken place. Football lads don't seem to have any rights. Imagine the outcry if this happened to certain other groups in society. No one's going to stick up for football lads though, are they?

Davie hated the Football Intelligence with a passion. They tried to get all chummy with the lads and tried giving you their first name as if it made you think they were on your side. The reality was that they didn't give a flying fuck about you or your family, they'd jail you any which way they could. It annoyed Davie no end that some so-called football hooligans chatted away to them as if they were long lost pals.

Davie didn't know why the police didn't use their football tactics on other more serious criminals. You know the type - rapists, terrorists, paedophiles, the lowest of the fuckin low. Imagine if they escorted members of ISIS everywhere they went whilst filming their every move? Imagine giving them a section 60 and jotting down what they were wearing and a physical description every time they set foot in another town. Imagine sending them letters or visiting their homes or workplaces at obscure hours of the day telling them to stay away from the ISIS meet and greet taking place at the weekend and checking up on them every two minutes. Imagine making them hand in their passports during any big worldwide ISIS events and making them sign in at their local police station. Imagine police turning up at their work in front of their bosses and colleagues as they had done on occasion to lads Davie knew. But no, this behaviour seemed to be solely reserved for the big bad football casuals of this world.

The day had been an unmitigated fucking disaster and to add insult to injury, Rangers had dominated the game, hit the woodwork numerous times, missed glaring opportunities and an almost open goal, only to concede a late goal out of nothing and lose the final. It summed the whole shite day up perfectly.

Davie had called it a day around 10pm, he'd had enough to drink and sniff and was beyond fed up. The day certainly hadn't lived up to his sky-high expectations. He'd been looking forward to it for weeks. He hadn't slept a wink the previous night for thinking about it and it had all turned to shit. Davie was just about to put his key in the front door when his mobile sounded. It was young Andy Paton. Andy was meant to have been in the pub with Davie but had been running late as usual and ended up in a different boozer with another mob of ICF, mainly the younger lot.

'You missed yourself mate!' Andy shouted. Davie didn't like where this phone call was going. Andy sounded as if he was fleeing out of his nut.

'We came across some Celtic, smashed up their pub and the few that came out got done, they were going down everywhere!' Davie had been out since half ten in the morning and he'd missed all the action. He tried not to launch the phone off the ground. Some Celtic had been done and he'd missed it. He tried to compose himself. Andy was still talking ten to the dozen on the phone. Davie closed his eyes tightly and tried not to let the large pulsing vein on his forehead burst.

'There was no polis anywhere to be seen man, fuckin magic! Got to go mate, we're still looking for more of the cunts!' Andy said before hanging up.

Davie took another deep breath and walked through the door. Laura took one look at him and laughed.

'What's up with your face?' she said.

'Nothing.' Davie said. 'I'm just knackered.' He was trying not to let his frustration show but clearly, he wasn't making a good fist of it.

'You were unlucky today. Thought they might have taken it to extra time, but I guess it wasn't to be. Always next time.' Laura said. This was not what Davie needed to hear at that particular moment. Laura knew fuck all about football and she was one step away from patting him on the fucking head with this patronising 'unlucky' shite. He bit his tongue before he said something he'd regret and moved past his wife to the fridge. He grabbed out a bottle of Peroni and settled down on the couch to watch anything other than the highlights of the fucking Scottish League Cup final.

CHAPTER TEN
When the fun stops, stop

After the disappointment of losing the final and more so, at missing the row with Celtic, which he'd heard wasn't half as good as Andy had made out, Davie was looking forward to a few upcoming fixtures which would have a good potential for violence. A small group of them were going through to sort Hamilton out on Friday night and then there was Hibs away, hopefully a good European tie or two on the horizon, plus there could be a decent domestic cup game thrown in for good measure.

In the meantime, there were lots of Saturday afternoon's when Rangers didn't have a game. They were either playing on the Sunday or early doors on the Saturday. Then there were games against the likes of Ross County and St Johnstone which didn't exactly get the old juices flowing.

Davie was meeting Andy, McKee, Billy, Clemmy and some of the young lot for a few pints as he did most weeks. Big quiet John Macdonald was there as well. Sometimes there were more lads out but more often than not it was this core group of half a dozen or so.

Davie had put his football coupon on in the bookies just down the road from the boozer. He'd stuck a score on eight games having three or more goals, a very healthy return of just over two grand awaited him if it stoated. He'd been close to a few decent wins more times than he could remember but kept hitting the crossbar, maybe today would be the day.

Davie liked a punt but not to the extent of some of his mates, he knew nothing about horses and only had the odd bet if there was a tip or it was a big race like the National or Cheltenham.

However, every week without fail he put on a football coupon and tried to win a decent sum. There were worse ways to spend a Saturday afternoon than watching the scores come in with some good mates and a few pints.

The drink was flowing and so far, the coupon was going well. Davie was beginning to think this could be the day for a big win. Billy McKay had also backed a horse at 25/1 which won, Wandering Willie, he'd liked the name apparently and the jammy fucker had stuck a tenner on it for a healthy profit. He'd taken great pleasure in telling the whole pub all about it. Davie had heard of bad losers, but Billy was even worse when he won. He'd been around the whole pub asking if anyone had backed the 25/1 winner and then when they said no, he'd whip his winning bookie slip out and force them to look at it. One wee guy had made the mistake of saying he'd backed it each way to which McKay had replied 'fucking liar!' before moving swiftly on.

For a change, watching the scores come in on Soccer Saturday was an absolute pleasure for Davie as all the 3pm kick offs he'd backed won relatively easily, the games he'd picked had plenty of goals in them, they'd been up with 10 minutes still to play. This was not what normally happened, usually he'd be waiting on last minute goals, or his bet would have been binned long before full time.

'Ya fuckin dancer, just waiting on three goals in the Man Utd game now.' Davie said.

Man Utd were playing Brighton at Old Trafford in the late kick off. Davie was already counting his winnings. This will pay for a nice wee holiday, he confidently thought.

'What's the cash out Wilson?' Paton said.

'I put it on in the bookies, plus I'm no cashing out.' Davie said.

'I'd lay a bit off mate. Stick a few ton on under three goals so as you win a few quid at least.' Clemmy said. Clemmy was a bit of a mad fucker but when it came to gambling, he seemed to know his stuff. However, Davie still wasn't for cashing out or laying off the bet.

'I could put it on for you the now and you can give me the dough later if you want mate?' Clemmy said, taking out his phone.

'Nah, you're alright mate, cheers for the offer though.' Davie said. He didn't fancy owing Clemmy a few hundred quid even if it was going to guarantee himself some profit.

Davie always hated backing something in the late game, he would never have taken it had he known it wasn't a 3pm kick off. However, Man Utd should put a few past Brighton plus they were leaking goals for fun at the minute so it should be a high scoring game. Davie was hoping it would all be done and dusted by half time to stop them all going on about how he could guarantee himself profit if he just backed this or cashed out that.

There was a wee young annoying guy in the pub who had been trying to join their company all day. He seemed like a little loner, in the pub himself on a Saturday. He was trying to get involved in conversations that had nothing to do with him and he was getting on Davie's tits. Plus, he had one of those faces, you know the type, you'd never tire of smacking the wee dick.

Half five rolled around and Man Utd started well, had a few decent chances and then Rashford scored after 15 minutes, and all was well with the world. Confidence was flowing. However, the Brighton keeper was having a blinder and he kept the score down.

1-0 at half time wasn't the greatest score line but Davie told himself that more goals were scored in the second half of games, not to worry.

'Is it two goals ye need noo big chap?' the wee annoying prick said. The wee dick knew fine well what Davie needed to win his bet, he'd been earwigging into their conversations all day.

'Aye.' Davie said, dismissively.

The second half started, and almost right away Man Utd got their customary penalty, superb. Fernandes stepped up, never in doubt, 2-0. Davie was drinking with a huge grin on his face, cocky beyond belief now. And to think they were all trying to persuade him to cash out or lay it off. Still almost the full half plus injury time to play and he only needed one more goal for a tasty £2054 return from a score bet.

'I'll get these lads. Looks like I'm coming into some money.' Davie laughed, trying to sound more confident than he was.

More drinks were sunk, and a few lines taken, yet still the score stubbornly remained 2-0.

'Don't count your chickens cause there never gonna hatch.' The Stone Roses had sung. The song was going through Davie's head which certainly wasn't a good sign. He knew he had counted his chickens far too soon. The game at Old Trafford was turning into a training match. This was beginning to look dodgy. Davie was quiet as he drank his pint, he was urging the ball forward. He knew he'd acted like a bit of a twat by thinking the money was his already and basically boasting to everyone.

'Here big man, hope ye get your goal, no long left noo.' The wee annoying prick was stating the bloody obvious. His voice was

47

going right through him. Davie tried to remain calm. Tried to get thoughts of flying for the little annoying prick out of his head.

The 90 minutes was up. Still 2-0 and still no sign of the much-needed goal. It wasn't so much about the two grand in winnings now, Davie had been gloating and acting like a bit of a knob thinking the win was a foregone conclusion. If the bet didn't come up, he'd be made to look a bit silly.

Five minutes of injury time flashed up which was decent, at least there was more injury time in English games than there was in the Scottish leagues. Davie watched and silently willed a goal to be scored. He wouldn't have even taken the Man Utd game if he'd known it was a bastarding late kick off.

He was rapidly losing hope.

Then in the 91st minute, Brighton got a corner, they swung the ball in and… GOAL! 2-1. Thank you very much.

'Ya fuckin beauty!' Davie leapt up onto a chair. Relief was the main feeling flooding through his body. Brighton had saved the day with that late goal.

'Fucking come on! I told you I shouldn't have cashed ou-'

Aw naw, fuck right off.

'Here mate, the VAR are looking into that, it might no stand.' The wee annoying prick better watch his mouth, Davie thought. This had nothing to do with the little loner cunt. Plus, he sounded a bit too fuckin happy about the whole situation.

'Hold on a minute, the VAR are looking at an infringement on the goalie.' the commentator said.

Davie had a bad feeling in the pit of his stomach. A right bad feeling.

'That's never a fuckin foul.' McKee said, 'Can't fuckin touch a goalie nowadays without a foul been given.'

The potential foul was being shown from several different and equally agonising angles.

'Here big man, ah think that's gonna get chopped aff.' The wee annoying prick was sailing far too close to the wind now.

A few minutes passed, it felt like longer for Davie. The longer it went on spelled bad news Davie thought.

The ref went over to the monitor for a look which didn't seem like a positive development. When this happened, more often than not, the goal was going to get chopped off. The ref also had 60,000 fans shouting at him to chalk the goal off. He watched it a couple of times. Then a couple more. This was fuckin torture.

No goal.

'I can't believe they've disallowed that.' Davie said to no one in particular.

The game restarted with 95 minutes on the clock, there would surely be another few minutes added on due to how long the ref took looking at the bloody VAR.

Man Utd had one final chance with what proved to be the last touch of the ball. A cross was fizzed across the box and the Brighton defender went agonisingly close to turning it into his own net, however, the ball grazed the wrong side of the post and went out. There wasn't even time for the resultant corner.

Full time. 2-0. Over 2 grand gone.

Fuck Man Utd.

Fuck VAR.

Fuck.

'Aw well, you win some, you lose some.' Davie said, trying unsuccessfully to put a brave face on it. He was fuming. No one was saying anything, they all knew it was a sore one to take. Especially with the last-ditch disallowed goal. That was just fucking cruel. Davie moved off to the toilet to try and calm himself down and get away from everyone for a minute or two. Eventually he'd be able to laugh about this he thought, but not now. Not tonight.

Davie entered the toilet and low and behold, who was in the toilet but the little prick who had been annoying Davie all afternoon. The little loner was stood at the sinks grinning away at himself in the mirror.

'Unlucky wi your bet big man.' He said, on Davie's arrival. 'There's always one game that lets ye down, eh? How'd you no cash out?' he laughed.

Enough was enough.

Davie cracked him in the mouth.

CHAPTER ELEVEN
Euro draw

Sometimes you had to wonder what went through the sports television company's minds when they decided on which football matches to broadcast. Did they really think viewing figures for Hamilton v St Mirren on a Friday night would be through the roof? Did they really think the fixture between two lowly and absolutely fucking brutal football teams would be a great advert for the Scottish game and get folk subscribing in their droves? The modern game really was fucked. However, the game would serve a purpose for Davie and a small, tight mob of ICF.

Davie hadn't managed to get any work done during the day. He'd been getting pestered on the phone and through email by the no toothed Celtic clad woman who was evidently taking advantage of her father. He'd eventually had to block her number. Why-oh-why had he given her his card. Naeteeth was becoming a right pest. His thoughts had been elsewhere in any case. Hamilton was the main order of the day. He'd decided to call it a day earlier than usual on a Friday and had met young Andy Paton for a pub lunch. Andy kept banging on about what had happened with Celtic after the final. It seemed to be his one and only topic of conversation, which annoyed Davie no end as he'd missed all the action. However, Davie couldn't help but noticing that Andy wasn't sporting any injuries whatsoever, so maybe it hadn't been as big a row as he claimed it was. Andy was possibly the unluckiest guy Davie had ever met when it came to getting injuries during rows which left many of the lads to call him by the nickname Second Prize Paton which, unsurprisingly, Andy wasn't a fan of.

After a lovely pub lunch of an old classic, sausage and mash, and a couple of right gassy pints they headed to the pub where they were meeting the rest of the lads. To add excitement to the day, not that it was needed, the draw for the last sixteen of the Europa League was taking place at dinner time. Rangers could get a right good draw.

Davie and Andy had thought they were the first of the lads to arrive in the pub until Scott McKee emerged from the toilet looking ridiculously pleased with himself.

'Thought I'd got my dates wrong; I've been in here for hours.' McKee said. He didn't look as if he'd been in for ages. He looked as he normally did, fresh as a fuckin daisy. In saying that, McKee never looked the worse for wear when it came to drink. He could drink like a fish for a full day and be neither up nor down. It wasn't like he was a fat bastard either and could just soak up the booze, he was just over 6ft and didn't have an ounce of fat on him. The hyper cunt never seemed to stop moving, maybe that's what kept him sober. Either that or he took a shitload of speed.

'What you wanting to drink mate?' Davie asked as McKee and Andy edged away from the bar to avoid buying a round.

'Two bottles of Bud.' McKee answered.

Talk about taking the piss, who ordered two drinks when someone asked. Anyone but McKee wouldn't have got away with it.

'You want a pint, Andy?'

'Aye, two pints for me.' Paton replied quick as a flash.

'That'll be fuckin right.' Davie said.

The three of them sat down and waited on the others arriving. McKee drummed his hands annoyingly on the table and his feet were constantly on the move. If it was anyone else, Davie would have told him to fuckin sit still. McKee must have been murder as a wean, his attention deficit disorder would have been off the scale.

Davie and McKee hadn't wanted a large mob of Rangers going through to Hamilton when they'd sat down and discussed it, so numbers had been kept to a minimum. It was just going to be the eight lads who had talked things through in the pub previously, plus Derek McPhee as they needed his minibus and couldn't very well ask him to drive them through, then leave him sitting in the driver's seat whilst they went to town on Hamilton.

Andy had texted a pal of his who ran with St Mirren's mob, the LSD, and asked him if they were taking a mob through for their Friday fixture. Thankfully, the reply had been in the negative. That had the potential to scupper the plan, if St Mirren had turned up and tried to have a go at Hamilton it increased the chances of a larger police presence and there was always the chance St Mirren could have had it with them before Rangers had their chance.

By the time the European draws were finally getting around to be made, everyone had arrived. They were all buzzing for what was going to happen.

The European draws always took forever, and everyone was getting impatient. Eventually, they came round to the Europa League draw for the last 16. There were loads of good ties Rangers could get. Roma, Tottenham, Sparta Prague, Feyenoord. Knowing Davie's luck, they'd probably get drawn against one of the only mob's that were still in it from Kazakhstan or some shite. Some fucking team from Moldova were still in it. No thanks.

The first tie was drawn out, Roma v Spurs. The next name out of the hat, or the big fuck off bowl that no one could operate properly was Rangers. Everyone stood up. What felt like ten minutes later, they were finally ready to make the big reveal.

'And Rangers will play... Sparta Prague.'

Nice.

Rangers had played Slavia Prague a couple of seasons back and one of their players had been racist to one of the Rangers players. Their ultras had put photos online with racist banners about him as well. Big bad ultras with flags posing for pictures and posting them on social media. Scary. This draw meant Rangers could have a good go at them or at Sparta, or at both of them. Fuck it, whoever wanted it. It was a decent draw relatively close to home and loads of the lads would be up for it. The last time they'd played in Prague away fans hadn't been allowed to travel due to Covid restrictions, so Rangers hadn't had the pleasure of taking a mob over.

The ICF were already buzzing for going through to Hamilton and the mood had been increased even more so with the good Europa draw.

However, that was for another day. Tonight, was all about Hamilton as McKee was about to remind them:

'The Europa trip's not for a few weeks lads so let's forget about that for today.' McKee said, 'We've got more pressing matters to attend to.'

Pints were being finished and jackets were being put on.

'Right lads, let's go and sort these cunts.'

CHAPTER TWELVE
Friday night in Hamilton

Davie knew that Woody and his mates drank in the Hamilton Vaults pub, not too far from the train station. Their shithole of a so-called modern football ground was a five-minute walk away. 2 Lego like stands and a fuckin tent for when the bigger teams came to visit.

Davie and 8 other ICF had taken Derek McPhee's minibus on the short journey through to Hamilton. They didn't want to be clocked on the train, the old bill might be interested in them or mistake them for St Mirren. The last thing they needed was any sort of police escort as that would put a swift end to any plans of violence tonight.

The drive to Hamilton wasn't like any normal football away day. The drive itself hadn't taken long, only twenty minutes or so. Derek McPhee was driving, and no one present on the minibus knew how he had kept his licence as he drove like a man possessed. He didn't seem to think that traffic lights or speed limits applied to him, no one could figure out how he'd passed his test in the first place. McPhee had stressed to them that under no circumstances was anything untoward to happen to his bus. He needed it for a big hire over the weekend. God help any Hamilton lads if they tried to smash his bus up.

There were no loud tunes blasting away and no big cargo. Everyone knew what the plan was, and everyone was more than up for it. There wasn't much chat or laughter on the short journey, everyone seemed focussed and ready to go. For Davie, this was personal.

The minibus was parked up in a side street, walking distance from the pub. The same side street they'd earmarked on the phone. It was dimly lit which was an added bonus. The youngest ICF there was Andy Paton. 19 years old. Eager. He would go into the pub first, make sure the intended targets were there and that the pub wasn't full of weans or women. Make sure they weren't going to attack a fuckin karaoke night. They weren't monsters after all. Second Prize Paton put his ridiculous and probably fake CP Company hood up against the fierce rain lashing down outside. He looked like a tool with the goggles on and he wasn't exactly being discreet.

Andy entered the pub. Walked up to the bar and ordered himself a bottle of Bud. The barman didn't look twice at him. He was practically bouncing on his toes in anticipation at what was to come. The pub wasn't too busy even though the game would start in about half an hour. A big crowd was not anticipated, especially with the terrible weather and the fact it was being shown on the telly. There didn't appear to be much in the way of CCTV cameras within the pub, only one camera that Andy could spot and that was directed at the till in case any of the staff were thieving. No sign of any old bill either which was good. Even the police couldn't be bothered with this shit mob. Andy looked around the pub and there over by the pool table was Hamilton's rag tag mob. There must have been about twelve of them. They were stood there in Stone Island jumpers and Aquascutum scarves laughing and joking. Embarrassing, after what had happened with Airdrie just a few short weeks before. After leaving Davie to take a kicking on his own. These clowns shouldn't be showing their faces in public after that, yet here they were bold as brass.

Andy had seen enough. This was going to be fun. The Hamilton lads had been daft enough to position themselves a good bit from the door so there was nowhere for them to run. No quick getaway this time. They had no clue what was coming their way. Andy slipped his bottle of Bud inside his jacket and made his way back outside to give the rest of them his update. The barman didn't see him leave.

Davie and the lads were still in the minibus avoiding the downpour and waiting on news. There were four youth and five old school ICF, more than enough to take care of these shitebags. Davie just hoped that Hamilton's mob were in the boozer, and it hadn't been a wasted journey.

'This is fuckin perfect lads' Andy said on arrival back inside the bus. 'About twelve of them in there, mostly older ones.'

'Woody there?' Davie said.

'Aye, he's there, laughing and joking.'

'He's probably laughing about Wilson getting done in.' McKee said with a strange glare in his eye. If he was trying to rile Davie up, it was working.

'He'll no be fuckin laughing in a minute.' Davie said as he left the minibus, followed by the rest of them. Davie hoped this would more than make up for missing the action with Celtic a couple of weeks ago.

'They're at the pool table up the back, can't see much CCTV and no polis about.' Paton said. He was nearly jumping out of his skin he looked that excited.

'Let's fuckin do this.' McKee said, rubbing his hands together. 'In the door, smash these fannies, then out and back in the minibus as quick as we can. No messing about.'

The nine ICF made their way towards the pub.

Who said a rainy Friday night in Hamilton couldn't be fun?

CHAPTER THIRTEEN
Revenge

'C'mon!' Andy said, a little too loudly.

'Quiet.' McKee said, glowering at him as they made their way to the pub's front door. The rain was still lashing down.

'Let's fuckin do this.' Billy McKay said.

Like McKee, Billy looked wired. He was holding his favourite little extendable baton, he didn't think he'd need it, but he'd reasoned that Hamilton were in a pub, so they'd have pints and bottles galore if they got a chance to use them and it made sense to have the little extra security with him. The thought of them getting turned over had never been considered.

'Walk calmly in lads, hopefully we'll get close to them before they notice we're here.' Davie said. There may not have been any police or much CCTV but most of them had hats pulled low, hoods up and scarves covering most of their faces. They had to be careful in case any police attention came their way further down the road.

The nine ICF walked in the door and immediately knew that their plan was out the window. The Hamilton mob had left the pool table and had their jackets on, no doubt leaving in time for kick off like the good little boys they were. They stopped dead in their tracks when they came face to face with Rangers. Some of the younger Hamilton lads thought it was St Mirren's LSD firm who had come in to confront them, but Woody knew better. He had spotted Davie and was on the back foot already. The wee cokehead runt decked out head to toe in fake Burberry had noticed as well. He'd gone a funny shade of pale and looked like he was going to pish himself. The nine ICF looked as if they were going to war.

'Lads, I've phoned the police.' The beanpole of a barman shouted knowing that trouble was in the offing. He was trying to bluff his way out of this. There was no way he'd phoned them so quickly.

'Better make it a fuckin ambulance you call mate.' McKee replied, wide eyes focussed solely on the retreating Hamilton mob.

Rangers moved quickly. The Hamilton mob had nowhere to go, yet still they tried to flee. They had more numbers than Rangers, but they had absolutely no heart for the fight. Absolute fucking shitebags, every last one of them.

Davie moved forward first and cracked an older Hamilton lad on the mouth. He went down far too easily. He literally crumpled in front of them. The rest of the ICF followed suit. Billy had his baton extended and looked like an absolute nutter as he whacked every Hamilton lad within range. McKee was going mental, and Davie felt a pang of pity for the poor Hamilton cunt unlucky enough to be taking a pounding from him.

One old jakey looking Hamilton lad was doing his best to put up a fight, he punched lucky Andy a cracker on the side of the head before Clemmy whacked him twice and he went down in a heap. Andy gave him a few kicks for good measure as he lay prone on the deck.

Another older Hamilton lad picked up a pint glass and threw it. Unfortunately for him, it smacked McKee squarely on the shoulder. It didn't even smash, just bounced off him onto the ground. McKee paused kicking the poor little runt on the ground who was no longer moving, then calmly picked up the glass before chasing the Hamilton lad with it. It was like something out of Benny Hill, the Hamilton lad started running full pelt in and out of the tables with McKee on his tail, pint glass in hand ready and eager to strike. Eventually, McKee ran out of puff and decided he'd had enough of chasing. He stopped and lobbed the pint glass which missed the guy's head by less than an inch. The glass smashed against a table. McKee turned and started on a Hamilton lad he could get his hands on.

Davie and Woody were now face to face. Woody had been a decent lad, always texting and occasionally phoning, he was a nice enough guy, but he'd invited Davie to the Airdrie game and then legged it with the rest of them and left Davie to take a pasting. This couldn't be allowed to stand. There were certain things you didn't do in life and running away, leaving your mate to get a doing was one of them.

'C'mon Davie, we're mates!' Woody pleaded with his arms open wide. 'I'm sorry about what hap—' Before Davie could even think about whether or not he was going to stick the nut on his former pal, big quiet John McDonald smacked him over the head with a bar stool. Woody went down like a sack of totties.

Hamilton lads were going down all over the shop. There were screams from a couple of women in the pub and from a few Hamilton, fucking big girls that they were. The sound of glass being smashed and fists connecting with flesh. Great British Friday night entertainment.

'The polis are coming! I've phoned the polis!' The barman was shouting or words to that affect. Rangers wouldn't be hanging around to find out if he had phoned them or not. For good measure, Billy McKay lobbed a bar stool at the big lanky barman which smashed a few optics behind the bar.

'That's what you get for phoning the filth ya prick!' Billy shouted before heading for the exit.

The attack had been quick. As expected, Hamilton hadn't put up any resistance whatsoever. They were even more hopeless than Davie had thought they would be. The little fake Burberry coked up cunt had taken a few punches and was now fucking hiding behind two women at a table further into the pub. His fake Burberry shirt had been ripped beyond repair and he had blood pissing from his mouth.

'Let's go boys, these fuckers have had enough.' McKay said, readying another stool to throw at the pleading barman.

Woody was left whimpering under a table, he had blood seeping from a gash just above his eye. It looked a sore one and no wonder, the bar stool had nearly cracked in two. Woody looked like he was actually crying. Served him fucking right.

Back in the minibus everyone was buzzing. It couldn't have gone any better. They were in and out in a couple of minutes. A trail of destruction left in their wake and no injuries on their part. Well, apart from Second Prize Paton who had a big egg sized lump forming on his forehead but that was to be expected from the wee jinxed bastard.

It had gone to plan perfectly. As they drove off, sirens could be heard in the distance. Davie took out his phone and fired off a quick message to his former friend, Paul Wood:

Kind regards shitebag, ICF

CHAPTER FOURTEEEN
Self-help for hooligans

'What are you in such a good mood for?' Laura Wilson said.

It was Saturday morning and even though Davie had been in the pub until closing after the trip to Hamilton, he had woken up with no hangover whatsoever. A result if ever there was one. He'd even managed to get up reasonably early and was making breakfast for his wife. Heavily burnt sausages and overly cooked beans were on the menu. He'd set the smoke alarm off but not even that could dampen his mood.

'Am I not allowed to be happy to see the love of my life?' Davie said.

'Aye, very good, what have you done? I heard you singing for God's sake and now you're making me breakfast?'

'I've not done anything.' Davie laughed. 'I'm just in a good mood. It's allowed now and again.' He was picturing the Hamilton lads cowering under the tables, his former pal Woody whimpering like a fucking big girl's blouse. He smiled when he thought of the bar stool smashing off his nut. It was always the quiet one's you had to watch out for; big quiet John was a handy fucker. It was no surprise to Davie that Woody hadn't had the balls to text him back last night. After the disappointment at missing the Celtic row, a Friday night visit to Hamilton had been just what the Doctor ordered.

'You want to go out for something to eat tonight, I'll meet you in town after I've left the lads?' Davie said. Laura looked suspiciously at her husband, like this was some kind of trap or trick he was playing on her.

'What are you after?' she said. 'My birthday's not for another couple of months.'

'What are ye talking about? I just want to take you out for a nice meal.' Davie said. 'Doesn't have to be your birthday or an anniversary to treat the one I love.' Davie hoped he hadn't missed another anniversary.

He would try and get her drunk and then slip in the fact he was going to book up for Sparta Prague away in the Europa league with the rest of them. If things went to plan, he might even get his hole, Davie thought before Laura stopped him in his tracks.

'I'm going out with Brenda tonight; we'll need to go out for a meal another time.' Laura said. Even when he was trying to do good, it didn't pay off. She'd rather go out with her daft sister.

'Okay, but don't say I never take you anywhere. Shout Olivia, see if she want's any of this.' Davie said, trying to negotiate the heavily charcoaled sausages from the pan onto plates.

'She's already had hers.' Laura said, knowing there was no way on earth that Olivia would touch what Davie had made, she'd already had a much healthier alternative.

'What about Allan?'

'He'll not be up for hours yet.'

'Oh well, all the more for us.' Davie said clapping his hands together. Laura didn't look too thrilled. The house was stinking of burnt sausages and the smoke Davie was producing threatened to set the smoke alarm off again.

Laura made some coffee whilst Davie dished up his dog's dinner of a breakfast. Cooking never had been a strong point.

'Must have been a good night at the pub last night?' Laura said.

'Aye, it was a good laugh.' Davie said.

In times gone by Davie had told Laura everything about what went on at the football and she used to love hearing the stories. In fact, she used to lap it up. But that was the eighties and early nineties. Now? She had moved on, grown up and she was forever slagging off football hooligans or tutting loudly when she saw some football related violence on the news. She was always telling Davie to grow up and get over 'all this nonsense'. She talked as if it was embarrassing for her to be in any way, shape or form associated with it. She hated hearing about some of his best friends and what they had got up to, whereas years ago she would have found it hilarious or a turn on. So, there was no way Davie was going to let her in on what had happened last night. There was no way she'd understand, and it would turn into another argument.

It was amazing the buzz you got after a good row at the football, it lasted a while and could cheer you up when all around you was falling apart. Not that you'd read about it in any self-help book; feeling low or just generally down in dumps? Grab a few likeminded pals, jump in a madman's minibus and attack a pub full of Hamilton Accies casuals, you'll instantly forget about all your troubles and feel nothing but good vibrations from the world.

Davie couldn't recommend it enough.

CHAPTER FIFTEEN
Football Friends

'I'll be coming up to your office if this isn't sorted soon. I've been trying to get hold of you but think your ignoring me. Don't treat me like a dafty, just get my da's house re-mortgaged, it shouldnae be that fuckin hard.'

Another lovely voicemail from Naeteeth. Davie couldn't even answer the phone in his own office anymore because, more likely than not, it was her. She had turned into some sort of mad stalker. It was a problem Davie could well do without, yet he knew there was no one to blame but himself. He was the one who had accepted the house visit, he was the one who'd said he could help them out instead of fobbing her off, and then finally, stupidly, he was the one who'd handed the tooth shy woman his card with his details on it.

Davie was just about to go out to lunch when the office buzzer went. After nearly jumping out of his skin, he reluctantly pressed it, fearing it was his persistent no toothed stalker.

'Alright mate, it's Murray, got a package for ye.'

Relief. It was his friend who worked as a courier. He must be bringing him the trainers and top that he'd ordered a couple of days ago.

'Excellent, come on up.' Davie buzzed him in.

Murray, the delivery driver was one of Davie's mates from school who had run about with Thistle for as long as Davie had gone with Rangers. Davie was forever bumping into fellow football hooligans in Glasgow. Whether it be just walking in the city centre or in a shop buying designer gear. Or even at the school's parents evening. Casuals or ex casuals seemed to be everywhere. A couple of times he'd been out with Laura, and she was less than impressed when he told her how he knew them.

'Alright big chap, how you doing?' Davie said as big Murray arrived at the office door.

'Aye no too bad, can't complain mate.' Murray said, 'I've got two packages for you today, business must be booming, eh?'

'Aye, just don't tell the wife.' Davie laughed, 'That's why I get all this shit delivered here.'

'My lips are sealed mate.'

Big Murray put the packages down outside the office door.

'Good job you caught me, I'm just going out for lunch, I'll walk you down.' Davie said, starting to move down the stairs, leaving the packages propped up against the now locked office door.

'You still been going to the games?' Davie asked.

'Nah mate, fell away from it.'

This wasn't the answer Davie had expected. If Big Murray had fallen away from going looking for football violence the world had gone nuts. He was always going week in, week out for years. Since he was a teenager. He'd been everywhere looking for trouble at the football. Murray may have been Thistle, but Davie liked and respected him. They had gone to school together and then fought alongside each other on numerous occasions in the eighties and then fought against each other in the nineties and noughties. Even so, there was mutual respect between them. Murray used to go down Spurs all the time as well for violence and now he had turned over a new leaf, given it all up. The world really was changing and not for the better, Davie thought.

'Never thought I'd see the day when you gave it all up.' Davie said.

'Me neither mate, but nothing really happens anymore, plus I can't afford to get nicked now, the wife's pregnant.' Murray said.

'Fuck's sake, congratulations mate. What age are your kids?' Davie was a little taken aback, he was sure Murray's kids must be a fair age now. Murray was the same age as him. In fact, he remembered being invited to one of their eighteenth's a few years back.

'22 and 24. And now we're starting all over again. It was a fuckin shock I can tell you.'

'Fuck me, it must've been.'

'Nearly crashed the van when she told me on the phone.' Murray laughed. He looked a bit shaken having to speak about the whole thing Davie thought. In fact, he looked a bit haunted talking about it. No wonder.

'Think I'd have been doing a runner.' Davie said, only half joking. Murray looked as if he didn't know whether to laugh or burst into tears.

'The missus is happy as Larry though, so I can't go getting nicked at the football now.'

'No, guess not.' Who could afford to get nicked at the football?

'In saying that, we're playing Killie in a few weeks and the young lot are nipping my head about going. I might make a wee appearance. One last trip for old times' sake before it's all happy families and smelly nappies. You fancy it?' Murray used to always ask Davie if he fancied coming for a row, but he hadn't taken him up on it for years.

Davie did fancy it, but he'd made a promise to himself after his kicking from Airdrie, he wasn't going to go with any mob other than Rangers. Plus, he couldn't go with Thistle nowadays, there'd no doubt be a couple of Sheep there if it was a big game. He'd never live it down.

'Nah, you're alright mate.'

'I heard you got a bit of a going over off they Airdrie bastards?' Murray said. Davie wondered how the hell Murray knew about that. However, Thistle and Airdrie had plenty of history together. Davie knew that Murray and the NGE were still sore about the big meet they'd had with the Section B at Arlington Street years ago when Airdrie had rightly claimed a result.

'Aye, last time I trust that cunt Woody. Did you no hear about our little visit there a couple of Friday night's back to settle the score?'

'Aye, I heard you's took a few through. Heard a couple of Hamilton took right sore ones.'

'Too right mate, fully deserved. Don't think wanker Woody will be getting in touch with me again after that.' Davie said. 'I'll no be expecting a Christmas card off him this year.'

'What you's got coming up?' Murray said.

'You know me mate, I'll go everywhere and anywhere. Got Hibs away next week but don't think much is organised. Then we've got Prague in the Europa. Taking a good mob there so should be lively. You lot got anything decent?' It was at this point, just as they'd made it out onto Sauchiehall street that Davie realised he'd left his packages outside his locked office. He was only going to be away ten or fifteen minutes, plus you had to buzz to get into the building so he reasoned it would be fine. In truth, he was too lazy to go all the way back up the stairs.

'Apart from Killie, absolutely hee haw mate, and nothing will probably happen anyway. No even been in touch with them. Always the chance we could get a decent cup draw but that's about it. Wish to fuck Thistle would get into Europe but not looking likely in my lifetime. A few of our younger lot done a mouthy Dunfermline scarfer with his own drum a few weeks back. That's what we're reduced to.'

Davie had thought that Rangers had a severe lack of action these days, but speaking to Murray, he was realising that he was lucky to be involved in a firm that still had the possibility to get into a bit of bother every season. Plus, Murray and his lot had never had the chance of any European trip, never mind a decent one. Maybe Davie didn't have it too bad after all.

CHAPTER SIXTEEN
Hibs away disaster

'This sums up my whole fucking week.' Davie said. He'd been in an absolutely stinker of a mood for days now after someone had stolen his trainers and top from outside his office and this was topping it all off nicely.

There were only eight of them in the pub. 8. In Edinburgh for a game against Hibs. Absolutely fucking shocking numbers. A load of the young Union Bear lot were also in the boozer but only eight ICF. No wonder folk gave it up.

They had taken small numbers to Hamilton but that had been by design, they'd known Hamilton wouldn't have had great numbers and let's be honest, it was Hamilton. Hibs were a different kettle of fish all together. Taking eight lads to Hibs away was a suicide mission but still they had gone through, hoping beyond hope that their numbers would swell as the day went on. It hadn't turned out that way.

Loads of lads hadn't made it or called off at the last minute. McKee couldn't make it as he was at his sister's wedding. Even then, he had nearly cancelled as he hated, and I mean hated, missing any fixture with even the slightest chance of a row. He had always been close to his sister though and he'd never let her down. Thank fuck he hadn't swerved it when this was all that trapped. He would have gone nuts. Billy McKay couldn't make it because he was down in Newcastle visiting some woman he'd been seeing or harassing online. There were also a multitude of other excuses, but as far as Davie was concerned, a few of them had developed Hibee flu and needed to have a serious word with themselves.

A poxy eight lads out and it was just their luck that they hadn't picked up a police escort. The one time when it wouldn't have been the worst thing to happen. It would have been a ready excuse to give to Hibs.

'This is a shambles, I can't believe this.' Davie said for the umpteenth time. Everyone was pissed off, but Davie was making it worse. They should never have bothered coming through to Edinburgh with such shit numbers, but the consensus had been that more and more lads would join them as time went on. This hadn't come to fruition.

'That's a load of Hibs.' Paton said, looking out the window.

'Where?' Davie said, trying to have a look.

'Down that side street.'

'How many?'

'Dunno, loads of them, about 70 or 80 handed I'd reckon.'

'Aw, for fuck's sake.' Davie said. Second Prized Paton was fond of an exaggeration or three. There was no way he could tell how many lads Hibs had out from this vantage point, but he wouldn't be surprised if they did have a right good firm today.

'We could have had a right good go with Hibs, no old bill or anything but were sitting here with fuckin no numbers.' Davie said. A few of the lads were rolling their eyes as he spoke, he knew he was pissing them off with constantly going on about the poor turnout, but he couldn't help it.

'C'mon, we'll have a go at them.' Davie said, albeit half-heartedly.

No one looked keen and who could blame them.

'We can steam right into them,' Davie continued, 'yeah, we'll probably get turned over but it's better than sitting here like fucking lemons.'

'I'm no up for that Wilson, that's a fucking bad idea.' Clemmy said. He was a right mad bastard, but even he could see it wasn't worth it. It was madness.

'Me neither Davie, fuck that for a game of soldiers.' John McDonald said. John hardly said two words at the best of times, so the fact he was speaking up now spoke volumes. Davie could see their point; it was just so fucking frustrating.

Hiding in an Edinburgh pub for fear of getting legged by Hibs. Fuckin embarrassing is what it was. 8 against 70 or 80 odd Hibs was suicide though. No question. However, at least they could say they'd had a go at them.

'It's just a bad day at the office.' Clemmy said. 'It happens.' When did he get so sensible all of a sudden, Davie thought.

'Shouldn't happen with us. This would never have happened years ago. Wouldn't have been allowed.'

'This ain't the eighties—' Andy Paton said before seeing this wasn't going to go down well.

As far as Davie was concerned, every Rangers lad and their granny should have been out for any game where they had a chance of getting at Hibs. Davie had taken a sore one off Hibs a few years ago outside Central Station and had never given up on any chance for revenge.

'That's Hibs phoning.' Paton said, staring at his phone as if it was about to explode in his hand like some sort of grenade.

'Turn it off.' Sensible Clemmy said, 'no point talking to them, today's a fucking right off.' A few years ago, Clemmy would have been the one calling it on with Hibs himself.

'We'll have more out for Aberdeen.' Andy said. There had been rumours going around that Rangers and Aberdeen were trying to get something organised for their upcoming games against each other, but Davie couldn't see it happening. The mood he was in, nothing positive was going to happen ever again.

'No point in organizing anything with Aberdeen if we can only muster eight bodies for Hibs away.' Davie said. Andy knew this wasn't an argument he was going to win, not today.

After the buzz of the Friday night trip to Hamilton this had brought Davie firmly back down to earth with a bump.

CHAPTER SEVENTEEN
Potential

Davie was still in a terrible mood. He just couldn't seem to shake it. The Hibs debacle had made him worse and that no toothed cow was still hassling him at every opportunity. He was also still raging about his missing trainers and top as the company he'd bought them from wouldn't refund the money. Davie knew the only way he would get any sort of money back was to say he never received the goods and that would only serve to stick his mate Murray right in the shit and there was no way he was going to go down that road. He knew he was the only one to blame in any case. He had been stupid leaving the packages outside the office and he knew, ultimately, that he'd just have to be a man and take it on the chin. If truth be told he was more annoyed about the whole Hibs situation.

Meeting up with a few of the lads in the pub had brought the Edinburgh disaster back to the forefront of his mind. He'd also agreed to take Laura out for dinner and a few drinks later that evening after he'd made the suggestion a few weeks back. The moment had passed, and he couldn't be bothered taking her out anymore. She was moaning her arse off as Davie had been storming about the house like a bear with a sore head for far too long. Hopefully he would be in a better mood after an afternoon of drinking with his pals.

Davie was still of the opinion that they should have at least had a go at the CCS even if they had got turned over. It was preferable to sitting in the pub watching them on the march and having to turn phones off and ignore calls but there was nothing he could do about it now. He needed to get over it.

Now there was talk in the pub of a possible row with Aberdeen. They'd need to sort numbers out for that. Make sure nothing was left to chance like the trip to Edinburgh. At least it would give him something else to focus on apart from fuckin Hibs away.

Aberdeen at home and away used to be absolutely brilliant, Davie used to look forward to the games for weeks beforehand but now it was a fixture which has been completely ruined through no fault of lads on either side.

Aberdeen was a place Rangers loved visiting and they would always get a lively reception. Aberdeen enjoyed their trips to Glasgow as well and knew it was always on offer. Some of the offs between the two mobs were great fun. It was a right good old-fashioned rivalry. Games with a bit of hatred really got the adrenaline flowing. The two teams didn't even have to be playing each other, like the time Aberdeen were playing in the cup and stopped off in Glasgow and it went right off at George Square. Rangers had been drinking in The Auctioneers and word had gone round that Aberdeen were close by. It was one of they moments that are few and far between these days. Lads on both sides got time for that and hardly even threw a punch. That was the downside of the whole thing. It was shocking the way football lads were treated but no one was ever going to stick their neck out and say so.

There was limited scope for Aberdeen and Rangers to get it arranged these days. The sentences handed out meant it wouldn't be for the faint hearted. So, organisation was always going to be key. No one wanted to see lads jailed, no matter what mob they were.

The ASC had done a sneaky one a few years back when they'd managed to get on the underground up the West end with no escort and get off right at Ibrox, but the police were quickly on the scene. Too quickly. The police knew they'd been made to look foolish and didn't take too kindly to it and since then the police measures had further increased. More often than not, these days the kick-off time was changed to 12pm on a Sunday at Pittodrie and Aberdeen got 500 or so tickets for games at Ibrox with huge cordons being erected making sure none of the opposing fans ever came into contact with each other. Where was their sense of fun?

Davie had thought Rangers were going to try and organise something with the ASC for their upcoming fixture against them next month, but it was now becoming clear that the idea conjured up by McKee, was for the two of them to meet on the weekend of the Scottish Cup.

Everyone used to look forward to The Scottish Cup but now it was normally just another weekend. It was a fucking crying shame and the blame in Davie's view lay squarely at the feet of the powers that be who ran the game. Rangers were at home to Alloa on the Sunday. Alloa at Ibrox on a Sunday, moved for tv - another glamour tie for viewers up and down the country to enjoy. Aberdeen had been drawn in the third round of the cup to play Queens Park at Hampden or lesser Hampden or wherever the fuck they play their football nowadays. Aberdeen's game was taking place on the Saturday which meant they might have lads coming down for it.

'Aberdeen always go up the west end or Maryhill to see their Thistle bum chums when they come here.' Billy McKay said.

'They'll probably no even come. It's not exactly a good tie that, fuckin Queen's Park away.' Davie said, he was still in a pessimistic mood.

77

'Aye, so we get in contact with them.' McKee said. 'Tell them to come early or stay late, catch the old bill off guard. They'll not even think we'll be out.' McKee looked like he had some sort of plan formulating in that manic head of his.

'No point after what happened in Edinburgh.' Davie said.

'Stop banging on about Hibs.' McKee said, 'Change the fuckin record, it shouldn't have happened, but it did. Nothing we can do about it now except make sure it doesn't happen again. Piss poor organisation but we'll sort it out. We'll have a good mob for the sheep, I'll make fucking sure of it.'

'We'd better.' Davie said quietly.

'There's no chance we can get a good off with them these days without the Old Bill finding us.' Billy McKay said.

'Positive thinking my man, where there's a will, there's a way.' Everyone looked at McKee. They knew he had been thinking about this for a while. They also knew not to doubt him. The vast majority of the time, if McKee said something was going to happen, it inevitably did.

Maybe the third round of the Scottish Cup wouldn't be a complete washout after all. Davie could feel himself getting into the swing of things in the pub after a few beers and he was finally starting to feel a bit happier with life when he realised time was knocking on.

'I'm going to have to love you and leave you lads, got to meet the wife.'

CHAPTER EIGHTEEN
Date night

Davie met Laura after he'd left the rest of them in the pub. He'd had a few pints, but nothing too heavy. He'd been trying to take it easy since he was meeting his wife for a meal. He'd laid off taking any gear so as he'd be able to eat something this time. On numerous occasions he'd been out with Laura or at a family event and he'd had to play about with the food on his plate or make up some excuse about not feeling too hungry. Laura knew, of course she did. She wasn't buttoned up the back. On one particularly embarrassing evening he'd arranged to meet her in a nice restaurant which would have been fine had Davie not turned up with white powder all around his beak. Laura had been furious, and they'd never set foot in the place since, Davie had thought the place overpriced and poncey anyway, so it was no skin off his nose.

Even when he was out with his wife, football violence was on his mind. He couldn't help but remember that the pub across the road was where they'd met after a row with Hibs years ago. Every time he was out for a drink with Laura his mind would be wandering. He was obsessed with football violence and casual culture. Alcoholics, Gamblers and drug addicts had meetings they could go to, maybe Davie should set up Hooligans Anonymous.

'My names Davie and I'm a football hooligan.' Everyone could get together in a wee hall and talk about offs they'd been involved in. We could give out wee Stone Island pin badges for every game you went to without smacking someone in the mouth.

Davie had let Laura choose where to go for something to eat. She wanted an Italian and that suited him down to the ground. Nice pasta and a few beers at somewhere not too expensive then up the road where he'd hopefully get lucky with the wife. Well, he was taking her out for a nice evening and plenty of booze would be sunk so the chances were increased.

His phone buzzed in his pocket as he sat at the table across from Laura. He discreetly sneaked a look at it. It was a text from Andy Paton:

'Sheep right up for it - next week looking good.'

A smile crossed Davie's face, superb. Hibs away would hopefully have been a blip, a disappointment that wasn't going to be repeated anytime soon. He had to get over it, put it out of his mind and move on—

'Will you put that thing away.' Laura said. Davie thought he hadn't been spotted reading the message under the table. Laura was like a fucking hawk.

'You have my full undivided attention.' Davie said, making a show of putting the phone away, but not turning it off.

They ordered a couple of drinks. Laura always wanted to share a bottle of wine with him, but Davie couldn't stomach the stuff, plus it gave him a right sore head in the morning, so he ordered her a large wine and a pint of some expensive Italian lager for himself.

Davie could feel his phone vibrating in his pocket again. He tried to ignore it and try to listen to what Laura was saying. It buzzed yet again. Then once more, that was three messages now. This could be important.

'I just need to jump to the toilet; I'll be back in a minute.'

'Aw for fuck—'Laura muttered under her breath but Davie was off before she could complain further.

He quickly looked at the messages outside the toilet. They were all from ICF pals telling him that next week was going to be eventful. This was part of the fun of it all, the build-up, the anticipation.

Davie was coming back from the toilet when he spotted someone he knew in the restaurant, it was that Football Intelligence fanny, 'Happy' Gilmour. Laughing and joking with his dog of a wife or girlfriend. Davie moved back to re-join Laura at the table. His mind was doing overtime, he couldn't get the image of that Gilmour prick laughing out of his head.

'You better not be taking lines in there.' Laura said as he sat back down.

'No chance, just the beer going through me, once you start you can't stop.' Davie was even more distracted now, it was that prick Gilmour's fault. Sitting there laughing and joking, probably telling the poor woman about his job following big bad football casuals. Probably telling her about finding us in the pub lounge on the day of the cup final and ruining our day.

Seeing the Football Intelligence in the restaurant had unsettled Davie, mad thoughts were going through his mind that the big lanky copper was watching him. He knew this wasn't the case as why the hell would he be on a surveillance operation with his partner in a restaurant, but these weird thoughts wouldn't shift. Maybe he had been followed to the Italian restaurant from the pub or maybe he was losing his fucking marbles. He was also getting distracted by his phone which was still buzzing every couple of minutes. Most of the lads who were texting him knew he was out for a meal with his wife, so you'd think they'd leave it be for a bit.

They finished their meal. Laura seemed to have enjoyed it, but Davie had to admit he'd been a bit side-tracked. It could have been beans on toast for all he had noticed. Davie was going to get the bill as this time it was Laura going to the toilet.

In a flash of inspiration, Davie moved across to a young waitress who hadn't been serving them. She looked a bit nervous as if she was new to the job.

'Could you do me a huge favour?' Davie said, 'My brother wanted me to organise this for him and I've messed it right up. You'd really be helping me out. It's his and his girlfriend's anniversary and he wanted to make it extra special. He wants a nice bottle of champagne, none of your cheap stuff, delivered to the table with a wee note attached. You got a pen?'

The young waitress looked extremely nervous now, as if she shouldn't have anything to do with this. However, Davie was talking ten to the dozen and she couldn't get a word in edgeways to debate it. She handed over a pen. Whether she would deliver the champers and the note was another matter. Davie scribbled on the paper and then folded it over a couple of times.

'He's sitting over there, see the big guy laughing with the dark blue top on, beside that old couple, that's him.' Davie said, the young waitress just nodded, still looking terrified.

'My brother will sort out the price for the champagne, maybe just add it to his bill, but this is for you, thanks very much for your help.' Davie handed the waitress a tenner and she looked delighted.

At that moment, Laura came back from the toilet.

'Will we get the bill?' she said, eyeing Davie with suspicion. Hopefully, she hadn't saw him hand over the tenner to the young waitress.

'All taken care of.' Davie said, smiling and trying not to look as shifty as he felt. 'Sit down and finish your drink, then we'll get going.'

Five minutes later, drinks finished, Davie and Laura were about to leave the restaurant when they could hear a commotion. Everyone in the restaurant couldn't help but hear the shouting. Davie and Laura turned to see what was happening, 'Happy' Gilmour and his 'girlfriend' were standing, a chair had been overturned and Happy looked as if he'd had a drink thrown over him. Davie's plan looked to be working better than he'd imagined. Fucking brilliant. The whole restaurant watched on to see what would happen next.

'Honestly love. it's nothing to do with me!' Happy threw his arms wide, his stupid looking hair was dripping, and his cheap looking blue top was soaked.

'Christine, will you be the new Mrs Gilmour?' Mrs Happy said, holding Davie's note. 'Who's Christine? What kind of sick joke is this? We've been married for three years and-'

'It's some sort of mix up, honestly, it's someone's idea of a joke.'

'A joke? You think our marriage is a joke?' Mrs Happy Gilmour looked as if she was going to leap over the table and smash her husband on the chops, hopefully with the bottle of champers Davie thought.

Unfortunately, Mrs Not-so-Happy left the champagne where it was on the table.

'Listen love, I don't know what this is, I don't know any Christine, honestly. I love you.'

'Is she someone from work? Is that it?' Mrs Happy said, she wasn't for letting it go. 'If you're playing away again then this marriage is over!'

Happy Gilmour playing away? Naughty boy. It was amazing the things you heard during arguments in restaurants that you'd instigated. Davie tried his best not to laugh.

'I've not done anything love, I promise you.' Happy Gilmour was getting desperate now. The lanky streak of piss was pleading with her. The whole restaurant watched on.

'Your promises are worth a lot aren't they!' Mrs Happy shouted. She looked as if she was wanting to smash her prick of a partner, however just as it was all getting very interesting indeed, the all-too-good-at-his-job restaurant manager intervened and seemed to calm the situation down. Fuckin spoilsport that he was. There now didn't appear to be any imminent bloodshed so Davie and Laura reluctantly left and made for the nearest pub to have a few more drinks. Once outside, Laura suspiciously eyed Davie who by now was grinning from ear to ear. Wait until he told the lads about this.

CHAPTER NINETEEN
Vrooooommm

Davie walked into the living room where Laura was messing about on the laptop. She looked a bit shifty.

'Got a wee surprise for you.' Laura said. 'I've managed to book a log cabin for your birthday, I got a great wee deal.'

Oh fuck, Davie thought. Here we go. He vaguely membered Laura saying she was wanting to book something for his birthday and here it was. Little did she know that he was going to be celebrating his birthday in Prague with his mates. Hopefully she had booked it for the weekend like any normal person and he would still be able to go with her.

'What day did you book it for?' Davie asked. He knew this wasn't looking good.

'Your birthday.'

'Aye, I got that bit, but is it my birthday weekend?' Of course it's not, I'm not that lucky thought Davie.

'No, that's how I got such a good deal, it's for the Wednesday and Thursday.'

Laura must've been able to tell this was bad news from the look on Davie's face, he never had been very good at poker.

'What's wrong with you? I thought you'd be happy.'

Davie was now booked up to go to Prague on the Wednesday morning, returning on Friday afternoon. There was no way he wasn't going. You couldn't knock back opportunities like this, no matter if your loving wife had booked a romantic birthday present for you. The main problem was that he hadn't managed to find an opportunity to tell her he was going away. In truth, he had been putting it off and the appropriate moment hadn't come up. He'd tried to tell himself that he was just trying to avoid another big argument, trying to have an easy life. In other words, he'd shat it from telling her and Davie knew that was pathetic. As Laura kept reminding him, he was nearly fifty for God's sake.

'Err, listen love, I've got loads on that week.' Davie knew he was going to have to tell her, it would be noticed if he just fucked off to Prague for a few days and didn't let her know.

'Plus, the lads have kinda... they've bought me a gift for my birthday, they've been...' For fuck's sake, you're a grown man, Davie thought. Just come out with it, plus the lads hadn't chipped in for any kind of present, he'd paid every penny himself and he'd even had to lend Andy a few quid so he could go. Money he'd probably never see again.

'Listen Laura, what I meant to say is thanks very much, I really appreciate it. I really do and any other time I'd be right up for it but...Rangers are playing away to Sparta Prague in Europe that week and I'm going. I should have told you sooner. I'd love to go to the log cabin as well if you can change the dates. If it costs any extra, then I'll pay for it.' This all sounded reasonable enough to Davie.

Laura didn't say anything. She just stared into space.

'I didn't want to upset ye, but I didn't think you'd mind since it was my birthday.' Davie said.

Laura still didn't say a word. Not one word. She did something far worse than get angry. A bit of an argument and a few days sulking and it would have been all over. A ten minute, screeching and spitting match and it would have been out of her system. But no, Laura looked absolutely fucking crestfallen. She even had tears welling in her eyes. Davie didn't know what to say to make things better. She looked as if she'd just been given the worst news possible. She'd had the wind taken from her sails. Still, she didn't say anything. Laura walked out of the room and didn't even slam a door or kick over some furniture. She went upstairs into the toilet and closed the door. Davie was sure he could hear her quietly greeting. Davie felt terrible but at the end of the day he'd told her and that was the main thing. If she could change the dates he'd gladly go and spend some time with her but if not, she could go with one of her pals or her daft sister. It would be a nice wee break for her, and she clearly needed one if this performance was anything to go by.

Davie moved out of the house to cool off in the garden. He sat down on a deck chair which had seen better days and thought over what the fuck had just happened. What a fucking mess. He was raging at Laura for her reaction, and he was raging at himself for not having the balls to tell her sooner. Why couldn't she just have had a wee bawl and spit at him but ultimately let it go like she usually did? Why did she have to act as if she was fucking heartbroken. What was that all about? It's not like it was the end of the worl--

Vroooooommmm

What the fuck? Davie looked over to where the horrible noise had come from. His elderly next-door neighbour was messing about with his lawnmower. Possibly the noisiest lawnmower he'd ever heard in his life. The noisiest lawnmower known to man. All he wanted was a bit of bloody peace and quiet in his own garden to try and calm down. To try and think things throug-

87

Vrooooommmm

What the fuck was he doing? His manicured grass was cut to within an inch of its life already. Davie put his head in his hands, tried to compose himself. This was not what he needed right now.

Vrrrrrooooooommm, VROOO-

Aww for fuck's sake. The old prick was really testing his patience. How was he meant to think straight with this old dick next door? There was no way any lawnmower should be sounding like that, fucking hell.

Laura would get over it, there was no way he could miss Prague, he was going and that was that. The thought of cancelling had never entered his head. He could try and get her to change the dates and they could still go to the log cab-

VRRRRROOOOOOOOOOMMM-

Fuck this for a game of soldiers.

'Gonna give it a rest mate?' Davie said through gritted teeth at the fence.

'Need to sort out my mower, think there's a few little kinks in it that need ironed out.' the elderly neighbour said. Davie thought to himself that this old dick needed ironed out.

'I can't hear myself fucking think...' Davie said.

'Oh, there's no need for that kind of fruity language.'

Fruity language? Who even talked like that? Fucking fruity language.

'Okay, let me put it like this, if you do that again, I'll bounce over that fence and shove the fuckin lawnmower up your arse' Davie said.

'I think you'd be hard pushed to get over that fence!' the old neighbour laughed. He actually chuckled. That was fuckin it.

Davie moved over to the shed and grabbed the rusted set of old ladders which lay behind it. The same rusted, crumbling ladders that had been waiting to go to the dump for years. In a rage, he set them against the fence and started to climb. This old dick of a neighbour and his fucking fruity language, he was going to get the loudest lawnmower in the world rammed up his fucking arse.

'Oh, come on David, there's no need to get yourself into such a tizzy. Are you sure they ladders are safe?'

Tizzy? Did people still speak like this? The old neighbour had a point about the ladders though. They made a loud, and worrying, creaking noise before they started to wobble back and forth under Davie's weight and the anger fuelled, clumsy way in which he was climbing them. The creaking intensified and the wobbling increased, then the ladders parted company with the fence altogether. Davie and the ladders wobbled precariously in mid-air. This was not good. Not good at all. Davie could see his elderly neighbour watching on. The old dick who had drove him to this. Davie swung round on the ladders and then started to fall backwards. He was going down in instalments. As he fell, he managed to grab onto the fence only for a panel to snap away in his hand. He kept falling and awkwardly collapsed onto the grass with a loud thud. The ladders followed Davie's lead and came crashing down on top of him. Followed by the fence panel. A few more fence panels looked as if they might topple as well.

'Are you alright David?' the old neighbour said, peering into the garden. He seemed genuinely concerned.

'Just having a right bad day, that's all.' Davie said, lying prone on the grass before lifting the ladders and fence panel off his chest. Thankfully, and remarkably, the only thing Davie had hurt was his pride.

Trying to smash the nicer than nice old age pensioner next door and then falling on his arse whilst breaking his fence, what a state to get into.

If Davie didn't laugh, he'd fucking cry.

CHAPTER TWENTY
Daddy daughter chats

Olivia was in her room feverishly working away on her homework. She was a right bright spark and was always talking about things that Davie had to admit he'd never even heard of. She was always getting awards and recognition for her schoolwork and would go far in life. Davie was so proud of her that sometimes he thought he might burst. He always tried his best to show an interest in what she was up to. At least Olivia actually spoke to him now and again, Allan never seemed to leave his hovel of a room and acted as if it was a real effort to say two words to him these days.

'What is it you're working on?' Davie asked, peering over her shoulder.

'We're doing a lot about places in Scotland and the history behind them.' Olivia said, not even lifting her head from the page she was scribbling on.

'Oh aye? Yer auld da knows all about places in Scotland. There's not many places in Scotland I've not been to. Come on, test me on it.' Davie said. Davie had been everywhere in Scotland all through following Rangers over the years. Olivia didn't look too chuffed with the interruption.

'It's fine Dad, I'm nearly finished. I'll be downstairs soon.' Olivia said. Davie peered down at her jotter to see what she was writing. She had the laptop all set up as well with a map of Scotland and some photos of landmarks. Changed days since he was at school.

'That the Falkirk wheel? I've been to Falkirk loads of times over the years.' Davie said. He was thinking about a row they'd had with the Falkirk Fear in the late eighties or early nineties outside Brockville. Now that was a proper old school football ground, a fucking health and safety nightmare, but a cracking ground with a great atmosphere all the same. There was always a good bit of bother any time he'd been. Fuck's sake he was getting misty eyed here. Their new stadium was in the middle of nowhere, had no atmosphere and summed up everything that was wrong with these modern grounds.

'Have you ever been up to the Falkirk Wheel?' Olivia said, dragging Davie from his daydream. The Falkirk Wheel? Old Harry Wilson who used to run about with the mob used to go dogging up near the Falkirk Wheel most Friday nights, but he didn't think that would go down well in his daughter's report.

'Eh no, I've never been. Looks quite good though eh? I know a guy who's been up there quite a bit.' Davie said.

'Yeah, it looks nice. Does your friend enjoy it?'

'Oh aye, he loves it. Was always going on about it, said I should go with him one time, but I didn't think your mum would approve,' Davie said, before swiftly changing the subject.

'Where else are you writing about?'

'Inverness.' Olivia said.

'Been there loads of times.'

'Really? Did you climb any mountains or Munro's?' Olivia said.

Davie climbing mountains or Munro's? He remembered being in a pub next to Johnny Foxes and McKee knocked the bouncer spark out, then all the doormen from the neighbouring pubs came rushing down and they'd had quite a decent row with them. That was until the Old Bill arrived and just about every cunt got nicked. Davie was slapped with a £100 fine for that and was told in no uncertain terms that he wasn't welcome back in Inverness-

'Dad?'

'Oh, eh... no, I've not climbed any mountains or that. It's a nice place though Inverness, we'll need to visit sometime. Maybe we could do a bit of hill climbing if you fancy it?'

'Yeah, that would be really good.' Olivia said. Davie could tell that his daughter was unimpressed with his answers to her questions and who could blame her? He got the feeling she was wanting rid of him.

'Scotland's got lots of interesting places, hasn't it?' Davie said, still not taking the hint.

'Yeah. Mum says you're going to Prague soon with your football hooligan friends. She said you'd rather spend your birthday with them than with her. I think she was a bit hurt.'

Davie was taken aback. Football hooligan friends? For fuck's sake. These words shouldn't be coming out of his daughter's mouth.

'I'm going to Prague to watch football, nothing to do with hooligans. My friends aren't hooligans.' Davie could feel himself going red in the face, he was embarrassed that his lovely little innocent daughter had even mentioned football hooligans. Why would Laura say that?

'Oh, that's good. I just think Mum was a bit upset, she said you'd done something to the fence and Mr Wingate wasn't happy with you?'

This was going downhill rapidly, Davie thought. He should have left and let her get on with her homework instead of having this conversation.

'It's nothing Olivia, your Mum shouldn't have said that.' Daft cow involving Olivia and what's old Wingate upset for, the fucking fence will get repaired. Old prick.

'Okay, Dad, I've got to get this finished for tonight...'

'I'll let you crack on with it love. If you need anything just ask.' Davie said. He was sure no further questions would be coming his way.

CHAPTER TWENTY-ONE
On our way

Laura had still been giving Davie a tough time about the trip to Prague and the fact he was foregoing a trip with her to the log cabin but there was absolutely no way on earth that he was going to change his mind and miss it. Her greeting and silence had ended and there had finally been lots of shouting and spitting over the past few days. This Davie was used to. This he could handle. The quiet sulking and sobbing he could not. The day before he was due to leave, Laura had eventually relented. She'd possibly realised that she was being a bit of a cow about the whole thing and ended up telling Davie to have a good time and to watch himself. Told him to have a good birthday and said they'd celebrate when he was back. She'd even suggested going back to the Italian restaurant they'd been to recently but there was no way that was happening after the incident with the Happy Gilmour's.

Davie wasn't a big fan of flying so he'd started drinking early doors in the Wetherspoons at Glasgow Airport. He had a good drink in him going on the plane and by the time the short flight was over he felt a bit steaming. At least he had made it there without making a fool of himself and revealing his fear of flying though. The same couldn't be said of Scott McKee.

McKee was so scared of flying that he had left days before on a coach trip with John McDonald for company. John was known as 'The Quiet Man' as he didn't say much if anything at all. He was a handy fucker in a fight but was murder for conversation. Poor John stuck on a bus with McKee who couldn't keep still for two minutes and didn't seem to sleep at all. The lads would take the piss out of McKee for all of this but not to his face. A few had made that mistake before and wouldn't again. It wasn't worth the grief or the anger. McKee compared himself to Dennis Bergkamp and his fear of flying and he also kept telling any of the lads who would listen that they should be thanking him for making the extra effort to go on the trip. If the tie had been further afield and required a journey by plane, then there was no way he was going. McKee's long-suffering wife had taken to going on holiday without him as she'd never been abroad in all the years she'd been married to him.

The flight to Prague hadn't been as bad as Davie had expected. The plane was full of Rangers fans so there was a good atmosphere on it, plus Davie had a right good beer in him, so time passed quickly. By the time they landed he was feeling a bit pished. The lads were all laughing as no one had told Andy Paton that Prague in March wasn't the warmest, Second Prize Paton was dressed as if they were going to Ibiza. They came out the airport and it honestly looked like it was going to fucking snow. Andy was wearing sunglasses and had shorts on with a little poofy man bag. He looked like a right tit.

'What the fuck man? It's freezing.' Andy said as they waited in the taxi rank. 'I thought the Czech Republic was supposed to be a warm country, this is worse than Glasgow.'

To make matters worse it now became apparent that Andy hadn't even changed any of his money over to Euro's. He handed Davie a Scottish tenner as his share of the taxi money.

'What's this? Where's your Euro's?' Davie said.

'I wasn't sure the Czech's used the Euro.' Andy replied as if it made complete sense.

'What?' Davie said, 'What the fuck? So, you just thought you'd take Scottish notes, and they would accept them?'

'Naw, I thought I'd change them when I got there, get a better rate. You know me, always thinking.'

Davie shook his head, he was sharing a room with Andy and he reckoned he was going to try his patience if this was how the trip was going and they'd only just arrived. Andy had spent the whole flight sleeping. The weird little fucker was asleep before take-off and didn't wake again until they were just about to land. It seemed like he could sleep at will. Then he'd got off the plane in his summer gear with Scottish money in his pockets, not a good start.

They made it to their digs to drop off the bags and the place had to be seen to be believed. The place looked like a fucking crack den. In fact, crack addicts would turn their noses up at it. They'd be fucking embarrassed to take their fix in there. Davie guessed that's what happened when you left it to mad Clemmy to book the accommodation. Cheap and cheerful, he'd said. It definitely wasn't cheerful, and it wasn't even that cheap. Clemmy was probably taking a right good skim off the money. The lads wouldn't be spending much time in the place anyway but there was a fair chance all their belongings would be nicked in this shithole. Davie had jumped in for a quick shower to try and freshen up and sober himself up a bit, but the shower was basically a trickle of cold water, so it certainly hadn't done the trick.

They swiftly left the worst hotel in Prague to meet up with a few other ICF, including McKee and a rather frazzled looking John McDonald.

'How was the trip, John?' Davie said.

'Never again. Never.' McDonald mumbled. Fuck knows what had happened on that coach, but Quiet John looked as white as a sheet and was saying even less than usual. He was drinking a whisky chaser along with a pint of strong looking lager which didn't appear to be a good sign. There was no way in the world Davie would have gone on a trek like that with McKee. McKee couldn't keep still at the best of times, never mind on a coach. Plus, he was like a social hand grenade. Some of the things he came out with were legendary and depending on the situation, very embarrassing. He didn't seem to have any sort of filter for the words which came out his mouth and he had the incredible knack of being able to offend anyone at any time.

McKee was buzzing around everyone, making sure they knew that it could go off at any moment. He kept talking about being prepared. He looked to be off his tits on something, but Davie had seen him like this plenty of times before. He hadn't taken anything apart from drink, he was just full of adrenaline, buzzing in anticipation at what could happen. He lived for days and trips like this.

McKee and a few others were now huddled around one of the pubs outside tables. They were looking at a map of the city which someone had either brought with them or bought at the wee shop next door to the boozer. Andy Paton had tried to show them the map on his phone, but McKee had sent him away and told him they were doing it his way, the old school way.

'This boozer's no good at all. We want to move to either this one,' he pointed at the map, 'or this one here. If we stay here, it means there's four different ways a mob could come at us. When we move to one of these pubs it cuts the ways of attack down. Means we'll know where they're coming from.'

Davie had to hand it to McKee, he may be an absolute nutter but in a previous life he must have been a war time general or something. He thought about things no one else did and most of the time he was absolutely bang on.

'Right, Clemmy and John, you two go and scout this boozer. Make sure they'll be happy with fifty odd lads drinking in their pub and they'll not phone the law. Davie, you and Billy go to this boozer here. Same deal. At least one of the pubs will be ideal.'

There was no point arguing with McKee, the four lads supposed it was a compliment in a way that he trusted them to pick the boozer. They set off.

CHAPTER TWENTY-TWO
Prague

In the end up they'd decided on moving the mob to the pub Clemmy and Quiet John had scoped out. The pub Davie had visited with Billy McKay would have been perfect, but they had some sort of speed dating night scheduled that evening. Davie wasn't sure the night would go as planned for the owners if loads of pissed up football hooligans turned up and then the pub was attacked. Billy on the other hand, thought it would be funny as fuck but there was no way either of them was going to take the blame when McKee saw what was happening.

Rangers had a fair idea that either Slavia or Sparta Prague would attack their new boozer at some point. The likelihood of violence on this trip was extremely high. No one who had travelled was daft or some sort of newbie to this whole scenario. Plus, McKee had drummed it into them constantly. Davie wasn't too bothered which of the two Czech mobs made the move, as long as they received some sort of welcoming committee. They weren't here for a fucking holiday or sightseeing tour.

Attacking bars was what most of the tin pot foreign mobs tried to do. Wait on the British mob getting pissed up, watch most of them leave and then attack the boozer with all sorts of weapons and then claim a result. Normally they were happy attacking bars full of normal fans. These foreign mobs thought it was a good result setting off flares in the stadium or stealing flags from scarfers, turning them upside down and taking photos for fucking Instagram. They weren't too keen on having a row with similar numbers or just going toe-to-toe with another firm who were more than up for it.

To make sure any scouts from the Prague mobs were in no doubt where Rangers were, Clemmy had tied up a huge Union Jack flag outside the pub which was emblazoned with the letters ICF. They weren't hiding from anyone. Plus, the locals were well aware of who was in town. There were Rangers fans all over the city, most of them were decked out in blue. Not one lad in the pub Davie was part of had any colours whatsoever. He hoped the Prague mob would find them soon and wouldn't turn over a boozer full of scarfers and claim a result. In saying that, the Rangers fans would probably get the better of the Prague mob.

The ICF weren't sure whether the Prague mobs would have a go at them tonight or on the day of the game. Either way they were prepared. There were weapons stashed all over the pub: small bats and extendible batons which Billy McKay and McKee had acquired from a couple of shops they'd come across.

A few of the younger lot had been keeping constant watch outside the pub and in the surrounding areas. They had been at it most of the day and were in contact with McKee who was like some sort of drill sergeant. He wanted updates every half hour and if they saw anything at all that was out of place, they were to phone him immediately. After a few false calls, around 11pm the call came through from one of them that a mob had been spotted. Those around McKee could tell that this was what they'd all been waiting for. This was the real deal. The youngster on the phone gave him more information. Around 30 of them, a couple of them were on scooters and they looked to be tooled right up. The youngster wasn't sure if it was Sparta or Slavia but who the fuck cared, it was a mob, and they were coming to have a go. Superb.

The word went round the pub. McKee made sure everyone knew what was going on and what was about to happen. Everyone stopped drinking and got themselves ready. They had been eagerly awaiting this news all day. The bar owner ushered his staff down

101

to the cellar. He had been happy during the day as the lads had all been spending a fortune in his bar but now, he looked tense. He had been assured his pub would be untouched but now he didn't look too sure. Everything would be fine as long as he didn't phone the old bill.

Davie loved this feeling, the old butterflies in the stomach. With the amount of beer he'd consumed Davie knew he should've been in some state, but he felt fine, in fact he felt better that fine, he felt alive. He was buzzing like McKee now, there weren't many better feelings in the world. This was why he kept going with the mob. This was what others failed to understand. Some people would never get their heads around it.

The young ICF lads who had spotted the Czech mob literally bounced back into the pub. They were out of breath and full of adrenaline. Everyone stared at them, waiting on the update. Eventually, one of them managed to get his shit together and shout.

'There coming now, fucking c'mon!'

CHAPTER TWENTY-THREE
Praha are here!

The ICF were well prepared. McKee wouldn't have let them not be. This was nothing like Hibs away. It was much more like it. This was what it was all about.

There was an emergency exit at the back of the pub, some lads were going to go out that way. There was a big window which folded down at the front of the pub, and the main door had been wedged open. There were around 40 ICF lads and every single one of them was well up for it. This wasn't going to be for the faint hearted. A handful of Rangers had also positioned themselves across the road from the pub, hidden from view for the moment, so as they could attack the Prague mob from the rear.

Rangers watched as the Prague mob appeared further down the street. About 30 of them, a couple on scooters right enough and most of them looked to have tools of some sort. Some of them had stupid looking red balaclavas on. The young ICF lads scouting had done well. This was no false alarm. Most of the Prague mob were right big fucking lumps. Not that it mattered. Davie knew in his gut that there was no way the ICF would get done off this lot. Sometimes you just knew that it was going to go your way. You could feel it in your water.

The ICF streamed out to face them outside the pub which would please the bar owner no end. He'd been deep in discussions with a few of the lads and had been assured his pub would be left unscathed. He didn't look the type to be phoning the old bill in any case.

The look on the Prague mob's faces was priceless. They had expected to be attacking the boozer, putting the windows in,

103

throwing a few smoke bombs, and smashing a few ICF or old scarfers with numbers well in their favour. It wasn't going to go down like that.

'Praha are here!' some big fuckin tattooed bear shouted, he had a stupid looking red gum shield in and black fucking UFC gloves on.

'About fucking time!' McKee shouted back, he was smiling like a mad man. McKee had feared that the Prague mob had shat it, but he was delighted they had made the effort.

'C'mon then, what you waiting for you Czech fucks?' Billy McKay shouted, he also had a mad grin on his face.

Some of the Prague lads didn't look as keen as the big lumps at the front, a couple were holding back and one or two were taking a backward step already. A good sign if ever there was one.

'ICF!!!'

Rangers didn't hang about. They made their move quickly and steamed right into the mob of Prague. The big, tattooed guys at the front were heavily tooled up but they soon met their match with forty odd mad Scottish cunts piling towards them. McKee, Billy McKay and a few others had extendable batons and were going to town on the huge frontline. Big 'Praha are here' was sparked out cold with the first blow struck and that seemed to set the tone of the row. In a matter of seconds there were three of them lying sparked out on the pavement. Big Quiet John McDonald had done one of them with a bar stool. It seemed to be his signature move nowadays.

A few of the Prague mob had seen enough and started to run, only to be met with more ICF who had now appeared from across the road. They forced them right back into the fight. They had completely underestimated Rangers and were paying a high price for it.

There were no Czech police in sight to save them from a tanking. There was no visible CCTV. Superb. In the middle of the fight, whether by accident or design someone had let off a big red flare and the smoke was billowing out everywhere. The scene must have looked like something out of a film, one mob smashing fuck out of another mob with bodies lying all over the street and red smoke everywhere.

A Prague lad wearing a red balaclava jumped on his scooter and tried to turn and flee but received a clothesline from Clemmy for his troubles, the poor guy's head was nearly taken clean off his shoulders. Served him right, should have worn a helmet. His scooter carried on without him and smashed into a parked car. The driver lay on the pavement. He wasn't moving.

Most of the Prague mob were now trying to flee. They were taking an absolute pounding. The main group of them were making it clear that they were not wanting to even try and fight Rangers. They had their hands up in defeat and were almost pleading for the beating to stop. Some of these tinpot foreign mobs had no heart whatsoever. They tried to evade the ICF lads who were still smashing them left, right and centre. A good number of the Prague mob had now made it to relative safety but had left their pals behind to take an even worse kicking.

After the Hibs disappointment this was much more like it. Davie was filled with adrenaline and took a moment to savour it all. This was fuckin unreal, not many people got to experience things like this in their lifetime he thought, before getting back to chasing some wee fat runt of the litter Czech cunt. This was a birthday he would remember for the rest of his days.

The big guy who'd nearly been decapitated by Clemmy when he was clotheslined off his scooter still hadn't moved and now one of the lads turned his attention to the runaway scooter. Some mad bastard had taken their lighter to it and set it ablaze. To rub salt into their wounds even more, a few of the lads lifted a red and white Prague flag from one of the bodies lying prone on the ground, turned it upside down and took a snap for Instagram.

CHAPTER TWENTY-FOUR
Comedown at the airport

Davie and the rest of the ICF had managed to get tickets for the game. A few of them, including Davie, hadn't planned on going anywhere near the stadium but it was reasoned that you never knew what could happen in these countries at games, it could go off in the ground or in the surrounding areas. Plus, they didn't want a few stragglers left behind in pubs whilst the majority went to the match. It would have left them open to being attacked. Rangers weren't even sure whether it was Slavia or Sparta who they'd skelped. Davie didn't know if there were actually two separate mobs or if they were like the Dundee clubs and only had the one mob.

In any case, the Prague mob had been nowhere to be seen before or after the game but some of them had been spotted in the ground. One of the poor cunts had his arm in a sling and Davie couldn't help but think that Billy McKay and McKee's extendable batons were responsible for that.

Rangers had somehow managed to lose 1-0 in the first leg of the tie at Ibrox. They had dominated from start to finish but lost a terrible goal and were now struggling to get through to the quarter finals. It was becoming a bad habit for them in big games, dominating possession, having great chances only to ultimately lose.

The match itself was uneventful, on and off the pitch but it had been enjoyable winding up their mob in the ground. The Prague lads present didn't look keen to even look in the direction of the away section. The Union Bears had put on a cracking display with huge banners and all sorts of pyrotechnics. Big Evans was raging to anyone who'd listen because he was beside some of the young lads who were holding red flares, he claimed that one of them had dripped onto his baldy napper and it hadn't helped when the young guy thought it was absolutely fuckin hilarious. The game ended goalless which meant Rangers were knocked out of the competition but by the atmosphere in the away end you'd be hard pushed to notice.

The rest of the trip was a right good laugh but there was no more violence to be had. If it had been the other way about then Rangers would have made more of an effort to get some sort of revenge, but the Prague mob must have thought better of it, plus some of them would no doubt still be in hospital.

Young Second Prize Paton had disappeared for ages after the game. Davie and a few others had looked for him to no avail, they'd phoned and left messages, but his phone was off. They were getting a bit worried about the little jinxed fucker when he eventually appeared in the early hours of the morning absolutely fleeing out of his nut. He claimed his wallet had been pinched. However, most knew that the seedy wee fucker had done all his dough in the red-light district. He was in some nick though and could barely string a sentence together.

The plane journey back home had been fucking horrendous. There was no other way to describe it. The flight to Prague from Glasgow Airport had only taken 2 and a half hours, but the flight back took an age. That daft cunt Clemmy had booked a flight that went via Amsterdam and took them nearly five hours. The long flight and the turbulence had made Davie's hangover ten times worse. He hadn't been too bad in the morning considering the session they'd been on. He was still buzzing from the off with Prague, but the flight had made him feel terrible and the few beers he'd managed to sink on the plane hadn't helped as much as he thought they might. However bad Davie was feeling was nothing compared to Second Prize Paton. The turbulence had completely fucked young Andy. Davie thought he might struggle getting on the plane as he was in some state but thankfully, he had made it. On the plane he hadn't said two words. The little jinx had been sleeping from the moment his head hit the seat but after the plane nosedived a few times, he was rudely awakened. He'd only had an hours sleep at the crack den hotel and when he woke he'd got right back on it. The wee cunt was absolutely out of his tree and had lost the power of speech. Davie could see him on the plane, and he looked in a right bad way. As the flight was about to land, Davie heard shouting and screaming and realised it was coming from the old couple next to Andy. The old lady was crying, and her husband was furious.

'He's been sick all over me and my wife, a disgrace that's what it is!' The old guy was shouting to the stewardess. 'The sickbag is right there! How did he even get on the flight?' he kept saying. In fairness, he did have a valid point.

He could see Andy holding his hands up in protest. He was trying to say something, but the words just wouldn't form properly in his mouth and then a little bit more sick dribbled out. This was all the lads needed after the flight from hell. The stewardesses were apologising profusely to the old posh couple whilst they tried to clean some of Andy's sick off them.

'Look at the state of him, I'll be making a complaint to the airline!' the old posh guy shouted. He was going over the score now, but his cream chinos had seen better days and the smell coming from them was absolutely fucking horrendous. Andy had produced a fair amount of sick for a wee guy and every bit of it seemed to have ended up on these old farts.

When the plane landed, Davie moved over and with the help of Clemmy, grabbed Andy under the arms. He was mumbling something that maybe sounded like some sort of an apology about the old guy's chinos. The last thing anyone needed was the police being alerted and meeting them in the airport terminal. Clemmy and Davie grabbed an arm each and just about managed to haul Second Prize off the plane before anyone could do anything about him.

The rest of the lads on the flight had done the off and headed through Glasgow Airport to the waiting taxis outside. This left Davie and Clemmy to deal with young Paton. Clemmy had somehow managed to grab a wheelchair when they got off the flight and now Andy was slumped on that. They must have looked in some nick. In a while they would see the funny side about this but at that moment all they wanted was to get the fuck out of Glasgow Airport. They hurriedly moved through the terminal receiving some funny looks. Thank fuck they only had hand luggage and didn't have to hang about for cases.

Some lucky ones had their own motors waiting for them in the long stay carpark. That would have been ideal, and Davie wished he'd thought further ahead. As it was, he'd have to negotiate a taxi journey home and deal with chatting to the driver whilst trying not to be sick in his cab. He felt rough and not usual Saturday in the pub rough but three-day bender to Prague rough.

Andy was a right state. The unlucky bastard had a huge bruise on his cheek and sick stains all down his jeans. Plus, he was sitting in a fucking stolen wheelchair. No wonder the nickname Second prize Paton was being used more often. One of the lads who lived near him thankfully had a motor at the airport as Davie doubted any taxi drivers would take him in that state. Big Evans wasn't at all happy at taking him but after much convincing he reasoned it was for the best.

'If he's sick in my car, your all chipping in for the cleaning bill.'

Having got rid of the liability which was Second Prized Paton, Davie jumped back into the airport and into WH Smith's to get some much-needed water and juice into his system. He bought a paper as well and it wasn't until Davie was sat in the back seat of the chatty driver's cab that he started to flick through the paper only to realise that the attack on the pub had made the Scottish news. Aw fuck, hopefully it wasn't on the television news as well and hopefully it wouldn't get back to Laura. For the sake of his hangover, he really didn't need any more grief from her. His head was bouncing already. He was trying not to be sick in the back of the taxi and this certainly wasn't helping. Davie read the article which was all the standard cliched nonsense.

'Shameful football casuals attached to Rangers caused mayhem in Prague before their club's clash with Sparta Prague. The thugs, many armed with weapons, were engaged in running battles which one eyewitness claimed was like a 'warzone'.

It went on to say that three Czech nationals had been hospitalised, one of whom had been involved in a crash on his scooter. Davie laughed; he felt a bit of sympathy for that poor bastard. Hopefully, Laura wouldn't see any of this. She had already been unhappy at him jetting off to Prague and then she'd started all this 'I've always wanted to go there' shite. She'd said on numerous occasions in the days leading up to the trip. Well, Davie knew one thing for certain; he was never going back to Prague in his life. Knowing his luck he'd probably get nicked for the pub fight or bump into some of their lad's intent on revenge. Davie just wanted the taxi journey to end. Get home and into his bed. The Prague trip had well and truly caught up with him.

CHAPTER TWENTY-FIVE
Uncle Freddy loves a bit of Prop

After Prague, Davie had been taking it easy for a couple of weeks. The drink and drugs he'd put into his system during the trip had fucked him and he'd even had to take a few days off work. Maybe he was getting too old for it all. His body was telling him to slow down.

He'd celebrated his birthday with a lovely meal in the house from the local curry house and Laura was being nice to him again. She had been to the log cabin with her sister and kept on saying how refreshed she felt. Davie's trip to Prague had left him feeling as far from refreshed as you could be, he'd felt at deaths door. Thankfully, after a few days he'd started to feel a bit more like his old self again.

After a couple of quiet weeks Davie had a family doo that he couldn't get out of. His mother-in-law was turning 80. She had never liked Davie and they'd had numerous run ins in the past. However, it was a night with family, so he'd try and make the most of it. He'd even chipped in a few quid for a decent birthday present for the old torn faced cow.

These family parties never were the liveliest of affairs, so Davie had sourced a wee bit of something to help things along. The guy he usually got a bit of gear from was in Dubai on his fifth or sixth holiday of the year, so he'd ended up getting a bit from young Andy who he was sure had charged him well over the odds for it. Davie was in the wrong line of business; he could only afford one family holiday a year and even then, it was a bit of a struggle.

Davie had just taken his first line of the night in the toilet of the bowling club they were in. He emerged from the cubicle only to see Laura's Uncle. Her Uncle Freddy was a bit of a tit. Thought he was some sort of gangster and always talked down to anyone unfortunate enough to get involved in a conversation with him. If you had done something in life, he had done it twice, backwards. Basically, the guy was a prick. A lying prick at that.

'You taking lines in there, Davie boy?' Freddy said.

'No mate, I wouldn't be doing that kind of thing at a family party.' Davie said, trying to fob him off.

'C'mon, jist give us a wee Patsy Cline, ya miserable bastard, I'll no tell anyone.' Freddy said. The smell of his strong aftershave was overpowering. He looked ridiculous in his long Glasgow gangster style leather trench coat. He also had more bling on than fucking Mr T.

'It's strong stuff this Freddy so you'll only need a wee bi—'

'Back in the day I used to deal in kilos of that stuff. So don't talk to me about how to take the old devil's dandruff.'

'Here, have a line.' Davie cut him off in full flow. There was only so much bullshit he could cope with hearing. He thrust the little bag into Freddy's hand. Knock yourself out ya fucking bawbag.

Freddy gave him the gear back via a mafia style handshake outside the toilets. The lying cunt really did think he was a gangster. Davie had a quick look before pocketing it. Fuck's sake, the greedy bastard had taken loads of it. Davie was getting a good dunt off it anyway, Andy wasn't lying when he said it was good and to go easy. Freddy would be out of his nut in no time with the amount he'd shovelled away.

The party was in full swing now and Davie had to admit he was actually enjoying himself, although Laura was looking at him a bit strangely. It was as if she knew or she had some sixth sense that he'd been up to no good.

Halfway through the night the music stopped and the wee elderly DJ announced the bingo was about to begin.

After the first round of bingo, some wee woman who looked as if she was at least ninety plus came up to collect her prize. She was accompanied by a younger woman as she could barely walk the length of herself. The whole thing was taking an age, suddenly there was shouting, Freddy had started yelling at the top of his voice:

'False call bastards!' The drugs were certainly kicking in.

'Let's congratulate wee Jenny McGlinchey on her win,' the DJ said through the mike, trying to drown out the heckling. 'Jenny has the top prize for some top play--'

'False call bastard!' Freddy shouted again, he was now standing and waving his arms about uncontrollably. You could see huge sweat patches under his arms as he flapped them about.

'She'll no have the right numbers; she's got fuckin Alzheimer's!' he continued. His arms seemed to be making all sorts of involuntary movements, they were waving all over the shop. He looked like some sort of sweaty nutcase.

Wee Jenny was thankfully oblivious to it all, she hadn't heard a thing as she was being helped up for her prize. Everyone else had heard though, they all turned to try and get a glimpse of Freddy who had by this point gone awfully red in the face. Freddy's wife Margot looked embarrassed beyond belief; she grabbed her husband back down to his chair. She furiously spoke into his ear, and he seemed to calm down.

That was until they brought the cake out.

All the grandkids, six of them, walked with the huge cake which looked like a home-made effort from some partially sighted relative. Allan looked horrified to say the least, but Olivia looked chuffed to be there. As Sandra stood up to say a few words, Freddy had wriggled out of his wife's grasp and started again. He was now sweating like Gary Glitter at an underage disco.

'For she's a jolly good fellow! And so say all of us!' Freddy bawled, 'Fuck me gently, it's like a morgue in here, it's a birthday party, no a wake!' What the fuck was in that cocaine, Davie thought, Freddy was going off his nut. He was a red-faced, bulging eyed, sweating, shouting mess and his arms were flopping about like mad.

'You no joining in?' Freddy enquired of everyone as they all turned towards him. 'Ya miserable bastards, it's her birthday, no her funeral!' He seemed to be stuck in this train of thought. 'Let's all raise our glasses and have a right good drink for Sandra!' he shouted.

'I think you've had enough Freddy.' Uncle Willie shouted over, he was 5ft 1 and built like a whippet.

'Who the fuck you talking to ya wee cock?' Freddy said with arms flailing uncontrollably.

Davie knew where this was going. Gangster Freddy broke free of Margot, showed a good turn of foot, literally leapt over a couple of chairs, and cracked little Uncle Willie a belter on the mouth. Poor wee Willie didn't have a clue what was going on, he stumbled and fell backwards... right onto the buffet table which was at that moment being set up. Unfortunately for wee Willie, he sent a bowl of pakora sauce flying up into the air which duly came crashing down on him and his immaculate suit.

Davie couldn't help himself, he burst into laughter at the crazy scene unfolding in front of him. Now it was a fucking party. A wee friendly game of bingo was turning into World War 3. Freddy looked out of his tree. Laura looked furious but then a few others started laughing at the sight of Willie. Even young Allan was pishing himself laughing. Davie hadn't seen him laugh like that for years. He had tears in his eyes, he was laughing that hard. Little and now very dazed Uncle Willie was covered from head to toe in pink pakora sauce and was muttering about how he'd just got the suit back from the dry cleaners that morning. He wobbled from side to side and looked very unsteady on his feet. He looked like he didn't know what the fuck had just happened. Freddy was being held back by two other relatives and looked like he was going to have a coronary. A huge vein was pulsing on his forehead and his eyes were popping out of his skull as he was led outside and away from causing any more damage at the party.

Everyone was laughing now, apart from wee Willie who by this time had been directed to a chair. As he sat, several of the women tried to rub the pakora sauce from his suit and clean the poor old guy up a bit. He was dazed and Davie almost lost it completely when he heard him mumble that he didn't even like Indian food. He did lose it completely when he heard wee Willie say that the smell of the pakora sauce was making him feel sick.

No one was quite sure what the hell they had just witnessed but the laughter was still going on around the room. Young Allan was laughing loudly and proclaimed to Davie that this was the best party he'd ever been to in his life.

One thing was for sure though, they'd all remember Nana Sandra's 80th birthday party for a long time to come.

CHAPTER TWENTY-SIX
Aberdeen anticipation

Davie rented some office space in Glasgow City centre to run his financial advisory business, Wilson Financial Advisors – a catchy, well thought out name I'm sure you'll agree. The office was based on Sauchiehall Street and had come in handy on the many occasions when he'd been too pished to make it up the road after a heavy session.

Sauchiehall Street used to be one of Glasgow's best and busiest highstreets but now all you saw were boarded up shopfronts and for sale signs. It was a disgrace the way it had been allowed to get like this. The rent on Davie's office had risen and risen but there was no way he was going to get rid of it. It was the only place he could go to get away from things and obviously he needed it to do the odd bit of work to make a living. However, the street was getting more depressing by the day and needed a facelift. In fact, it needed a fucking miracle. Soon enough, Davie would be the last business left on the famous street.

Davie had run his own company for a good few years now. He felt he was reasonably successful. He made enough to get by in any case. There was no way he could go back to working for someone else now, being self-employed suited him down to the ground. Davie knew guys from all walks of life who had been part of mobs at the football. That's why he always laughed at the 'mindless thugs' slur that always appeared in the media. The media would never admit that successful people were football hooligans. Business owners were hooligans. Guys who employed loads of people and pumped millions of pounds into the economy, regularly went out on a Saturday looking for bother.

Davie had to admit that he enjoyed going to his work even though it got a bit lonely sometimes. He had brought most of his albums to the office after Laura had moaned her arse off about the mess he'd made with them and how they took up too much room. She wanted him to get a Spotify account or use a fucking Alexa for music. She said no one used a CD player anymore. She hadn't been pleased when he said she should be thankful he wasn't into vinyl like a couple of his mates.

Davie had even built a wardrobe and he kept a lot of his jackets here. And trainers. There were dozens of pairs lying around the place, some of them had hardly ever been worn. If Laura knew what he'd spent on the clothes and trainers she'd go mental. Thankfully, she never dropped by for any unexpected visits.

He spent lots of time in the office. Laura thought he must be working hard with all the extra hours he was putting in, but it wasn't reflected in his pay packet. Today he was listening to The Charlatans 'Tellin Stories' - what a fuckin album. He'd seen them a few times at the Barra's which was always top class.

Davie had loads of books in the office as well and not just books about football hooligans, although there were loads. In fact, it was an extensive collection of football hooligan books, some good, some not so good and some downright hilarious.

He regularly watched a few different football hooligan films as well. ID, The Firm and the Football factory were class. Green Street was that bad it was actually funny. Davie had never been to an off with one of the lads dressed in full pilot uniform. He'd watched it back last year and couldn't believe how bad it was.

Today, in between doing some actual work, he was watching old offs on YouTube, some of which he had taken part in. He was also talking to some of the lads on WhatsApp about the upcoming

Aberdeen meet. He had turned being a football hooligan into an all-consuming passion. Many people, including Laura every weekend, asked him 'Are you never going to grow up?' Some people had mid-life crisis's and bought fancy sports cars, Davie liked to put on a nice Paul & Shark and have a row at the football with other like-minded individuals. Was that really the crime of the century?

The anticipation of a big game was all part of the fun. Although this time they weren't even playing each other which made it even more risky. Often the game or potential for violence got talked up so much that it was almost certain to be a disappointment when it actually arrived.

Lots of things needed to be sorted for Aberdeen. Travel - how would a decent sized mob of ICF get through to the pub without picking up an unwanted police escort? Minibuses? Cars? Taxis? Location - would they go straight to the meeting place or try and get close and then make contact from there. Was there a pub they could all go to that wouldn't panic and phone the old bill when 50 odd football hooligans arrived unannounced?

These WhatsApp groups were a good way to pass the time but sometimes Davie had missed out on hours of work as he'd got caught up in conversations or arguments. Some of the younger ones must have absolutely no time to do anything worthwhile at all, they were on Instagram, WhatsApp, snapchat, Facebook, and fuck knows where else. Thank God he was married, some of his mates spent hours on apps trying to find women.

Davie checked his messages on the office phone. Only one and it was yet another abusive voicemail from Naeteeth. Did he have any real clients these days?

'Listen you ya fuckin bellend bastard, I'm warning ye for the last time… ma dad needs his house selt and you better help ya dafty. Phone me back oan this number or I'll come doon tae your office again.'

Again? That was a bit worrying. What a charming woman she was. However, she was becoming a hassle he could do without. She was practically stalking him. Phone messages at the office, text messages on the mobile and constant phone calls. He had blocked her number twice now, but the toothless cow was still managing to get through. She was like some sort of no toothed IT wizard. It was beyond a joke now. He was going to have to deal with her. Get her some sort of deal or try and pass her off to someone who could help her. Davie would say one thing for the no toothed cow, she was persistent.

CHAPTER TWENTY-SEVEN
Gardening Leave

Davie had invited Andy Paton around to help him fix the fence which he had inadvertently broken whilst trying to attack his elderly neighbour. Young Second Prize seemed to be permanently in-between jobs. The reality of the situation was that he was one lazy bastard of a boy and would rather lay in his bed playing fucking computer games than go out to make an honest living. Davie had expected him at the house at 10, Andy turned up at 11 which wasn't too bad for him. At least he had shown up.

'What the fuck was in that charlie mate?' Davie said as they made their way around the side of the house to the garden.

'It's the business, ain't it?' Andy said.

'My wife's Uncle Freddy took a good bit of it and went off his nut, smacked her wee old Uncle Willie on the chops and then took the front door off the hinges when he was being escorted out.'

'Fucking hell, what age is her Uncle?'

'I dunno, sixty odds.'

'Aw whit, don't be giving prop you get from me to old relative's mate, he's lucky he never had a heart attack. Is he alright?' Paton said.

'Aye, apart from making a show of himself. I don't think he slept for a few days either but he's brand new now. He's a prick anyway mate so don't worry about it.'

'What happened to the fence?' Andy said, inspecting the damage. 'The weather's not been that bad.'

'A couple of panel's just fell off, wear and tear I reckon.' Davie said.

'It doesn't look that old, panels shouldn't just be breaking off.'

'If you want to know the truth, it was me. I broke a bit of the fence trying to climb it to batter the old neighbour next door.'

'Fucking hell' Andy laughed, 'I take it that's the old guy who keeps looking at us from the window over there?'

'Aye, that would be him.'

'Nosey old prick, we should give him something to tell the neighbourhood watch group about.'

'It's not worth it. Let's just get this fixed and stop the old fucker from moaning about it. You want anything to drink?'

'Aye, a wee Red Bull or a juice wouldn't go amiss. Or even a wee latte if you've got that?'

Andy was onto plums. Red Bull or a latte? Where did he think he was? Davie went off to sort out a glass of water or a coke whilst Andy surveyed the fence, it didn't look like a hard job and wouldn't take them long. He noticed the old neighbour was still peeking out at him behind the curtains. Andy thought he would have a little fun.

Davie was in the kitchen sorting out the drinks when he heard the scream. A loud, high-pitched scream, followed by shouting. It took him a moment to realise it was coming from his back garden. This was not good.

'Aw for fuck's sake…'

Andy was up the little step ladder he had brought looking at the fence. The only thing was though, he was bollock naked. His elderly neighbour had come out to see what he was playing at. However, before he had made it down the stairs, his equally elderly wife was coming back in with a couple of bags of shopping. She had seen a naked man standing on a step ladder looking at her over the fence, dropped her shopping and screamed at the top of her lungs. She looked like she needed a lie down.

'What is going on here David?' the old dick said.

'I've no idea what is going on. Is your wife okay?' Davie said. His wife did not look well at all.

'She's had a terrible shock seeing this! Plus, she's smashed a jar of pickles!'

Andy was still stood with absolutely nothing on but now he was laughing that hard he could barely speak. Through the laughter Davie was sure he heard him splutter about 'fucking pickles'. Davie grabbed him down from the step ladder.

'Put on some fuckin clothes.' Davie said, Andy grabbed his clothes and started to slowly put them back on, he could hardly breathe he was laughing so much.

'I don't expect to look out my window and see a naked man up a step ladder and Elsie shouldn't have to get a shock like that. He could've killed her!'

Davie was now trying hard not to laugh.

'I'm sorry for this, I hope Elsie gets over the shock.' Davie said.

'I'd maybe be inclined to accept your apology if you weren't smiling like a bloody Cheshire cat!'

'Now, now, there's no need for any of that fruity language.' Davie said. Andy was howling now. He had managed to get his pants and socks back on but almost fell over as he tried to negotiate his jeans.

'C'mon Elsie, let's get you back inside. You're lucky I'm not phoning the police!'

Davie and Andy were both now laughing hard as the elderly couple made their way back inside.

'I left you for two minutes ya prick.' Davie said.

'Sorry mate, just thought I'd put on a wee show for the nosey bastard.'

CHAPTER TWENTY-EIGHT
Scare

Laura was sat on the couch. In silence. Even the television was turned off. She was just staring into space.

'You alright?' Davie said. She didn't look alright.

'What?' Laura said, just noticing that Davie had entered the room and asked her something.

'I said, are you alright?' Davie tried again.

Laura burst into tears. What the fuck? Davie was sure he hadn't done anything to upset her. In fact, he was certain, oh fuck maybe she'd found out about the row in Prague or about him giving her Uncle Freddy gear. Or about Andy being naked in the garden. It couldn't be any of that though, there would be shouting and spitting surely, not tears. He moved across to the couch and tried to console her. He awkwardly rubbed at her arm.

'What's wrong? C'mon, it's no that bad.' Davie said, awkwardly patting her on the back now.

'I think I might be pregnant.' Laura said.

'Aww you're fucking joking!' Davie said before he could catch himself. He had also stood up and moved away from her as if she had the plague.

'What a lovely thing to say.' Laura said, tears streaming down her cheeks.

'I'm sorry but fucking hell, it's just a bit of a shock.' Davie said, trying to process what the hell was going on.

'You think I'm happy about this? I'm 46 years old, I thought I was too old for any more kids, I didn't think I even could-'

'Are you not still on the pill?' Davie asked.

'Yes, I'm still on the-'

'Well, how could this have happened? We've had sex once in about two year and you might be pregnant? Fuck me.' Davie wasn't handling this unexpected news well at all.

'What you want me to say? I'm not exactly jumping for joy, am I?' Laura said.

'Have you taken a test?'

'Not yet.'

'Well, what are ye waiting for?'

'I've not got any.' Laura said.

'Where's my car keys?'

Davie jumped in the car and drove to the local supermarket in a time even Lewis Hamilton would've been proud of. His mind was a blur, how could this even be happening? He'd hardly been near Laura. That night out had been a costly mistake. He must have super sperm or something. He thought back to his conversation with that poor cunt Murray from Thistle who was having another wean and had grown up kids. He was regretting laughing at his old mate's plight and now he was paying a hefty price. There was no way this could happen to Davie and Laura, no fucking way.

Davie abandoned the car in a disabled space and sprinted into Asda. He found the aisle he was looking for. There were too many options, he picked up three different makes of test and headed for the self-service check outs.

'Wilson! How you doing mate?' Why is it when you don't want to meet anyone you know, you always bump into someone.

'Wilson, you still going to the fitba?' Wee Frankie Mitchell looked to be buzzing out of his tits, fuck knows what he was on, but his eyes were going in different directions, and he was sweating more than any normal human should.

'Aye mate, still going, how's tricks with you?' Davie said, trying to put the tests away in a carrier bag that wouldn't fucking open at the self-service check out that was making funny noises. Wee Frankie was an alright lad, but the last thing Davie needed right now was to be standing in the middle of a supermarket chatting for ages, especially with the wee man in a state like this.

'Canny complain my man, I've been out for a few days mate, bit of a mad bender. I canny even remember what the fuck I came in here for. Probably for a cargo though, eh big man!' Frankie laughed, 'I'm no coming in for any of they tests you've got there, I can tell ye that for nothing! You should have got the snip mate!' Wee Frankie was talking ten to the dozen. Even though he was absolutely smashed and wired to the moon, he was right - he should have got the snip. He hadn't even considered it but after all of this he'd make it a top priority.

'Have a good one Frankie mate, I better go.' Davie said, trying to end the conversation.

'Too right mate, I'll no say anything about the old preggers tests! Take care pal, see you soon. Hope it all works out well!'

'Aye, me too mate.' Davie hurried out of the supermarket and back to his shabbily parked car. There was some fat woman peering into his car as he approached.

'You're not disabled!' the fat woman was shouting at him.

'You don't know anything about me love, so fuck off, eh?' Davie said, opening the door. He didn't have time for this pish.

'Who do...Well, I never, Who do you think you are?'

'I'm your fucking dietician ya fat cow, now get out of my way!' Davie was in no mood for niceties. He closed the car door and sped off, leaving the heavy woman speechless.

This is what he got for making fun of his big mate Murray who was expecting another kid. He should have kept his stupid thoughts to himself.

Davie made it home in record time and blootered his way through the front door. He thrust the bag with the pregnancy tests at Laura. If he wasn't careful, he was going to have a fucking heart attack.

Laura went away to pee on a pregnancy test or three, or whatever it was you did with the things these days and Davie sat down and seriously thought about praying. Please let it be negative. As Laura kept on reminding him, Davie was nearly fifty. He couldn't start again with a kid, no way. They were just getting to a good stage in life now, the kids basically looked after themselves and- No. No way. No way was he going back to sleepless nights, changing shitty nappies and constant fuckin worry. No. It's going to be negative, it's fucking got to be, Davie thought.

As Davie was pacing up and down, now thinking about packing his bags and possible divorce, Laura reappeared on stairs.

'Well?' Davie said.

'You need to wait a few minutes.'

Davie was now pacing up and down the living room at a frantic pace. This was torture.

'Oh, thank God!' Laura said.

'What? What is it?' Davie said, louder than he had meant.

'Negative.'

Davie sat down.

He felt shattered.

Relief flooded through his body.

Thank fuck for that.

CHAPTER TWENTY-NINE
Organisation is key

Aberdeen's ASC and Rangers ICF lads had been texting back and forth all morning. The day had finally arrived. Aberdeen always loved having a pop at Rangers and they seemed to be right up for it. Good. At least the day wasn't going to be a washout or a non-event. There was nothing worse than looking forward to a potential row for ages, planning it through and then for absolutely nothing to happen. Okay, getting done in was probably worse or getting the jail, but a complete non-event was up there.

Today had been organised well and hopefully the football intelligence or old bill wouldn't get wind of the plans. There would be a few decent sentences dished out if lads were caught for this but there was no point in thinking like that.

McKee and one of Aberdeen's Glasgow based lads who he had known for years had met up on the Thursday night to look at the potential location for the arranged meet. Both seemed to think it could work. Some people found it strange that two lads from opposing mobs could meet up, even be friends and then try and beat the shit out of each other later on, but at the end of the day we all had loads in common and no one wanted to see any arrests on either side.

The main thing which would fuck the possible meet up was people being mouthy, so plans were being kept as secretive as possible, loose lips sink ships after all, as McKee was fond of saying. Also, numbers were to be kept reasonable on both sides. No more than fifty lads a side had been agreed. Both mobs knew it didn't matter, the two firms would go for it with any amount, outnumbered or not.

Aberdeen lads were holed up in a shithole of a boozer in Maryhill with no police escort. The pub owner knew the score, as long as his pub didn't get smashed up and he made a few quid he was happy and wouldn't phone the law. Most of the Aberdeen lot hadn't even gone to their cup tie against Queens Park earlier in the day for fear of attracting police attention.

Rangers lads were in a pub near Ibrox and the plan was for them to leave in small groups to a pub five minutes away from the ASC. Rangers were leaving in cars and taxis, and this would hopefully eliminate any CCTV being produced at a later date. McKee had been trying to get McPhee to bring his minibus but had been told in no uncertain terms that there was no chance as he needed it for a good paying job in the morning and he couldn't risk it getting smashed up or impounded.

If the police did make any arrests, lads would have to claim they had bumped into each other by coincidence, it wasn't the best excuse, but it would have to do if it came down to it. There was no way they could know for certain that the row had been well organised in advance.

The pub the ICF made their way to wasn't much kop either but for what Rangers had planned it was perfect. The pub owner seemed pleased at his upturn in trade as more and more ICF lads entered the premises. Before they'd arrived there had only been a handful of old punters in attendance. Every Rangers lad had made it and there hadn't been a sniff of old bill interference anywhere.

McKee made the phone call to his ASC pal.

'That's us here. Everything okay your end?' McKee said.

'Everything looking good here mate. You ready for this?' the Aberdeen lad said.

'Fuck off with that pish.' McKee wasn't one for much small talk. 'Make a move at 8, it'll take us both a couple of minutes to bump into each other where we said on Thursday. Tell your lads to keep the fuckin noise down on the way there.'

'We'll be fine. See you in half an hour.' The call was ended.

You could feel the buzz around the pub. It was electric. Everyone looked up for it. If you couldn't get yourself up for this, then you were in the wrong game. Davie couldn't keep still. There were always a few nerves before you knew it was going to kick off but the old butterflies in the stomach was a good thing. Kept you on your toes. If this went the way it was supposed to, then there'd be a right good off, no one would get the nick and Rangers would smash the sheepshagging bastards everywhere.

McKee went round everyone, telling them to be ready to leave at 8 sharp, it was only a few minutes away now. Davie hadn't had much to drink, he liked to keep a clear head when he knew the chances of an off were high. He got the feeling he'd need his wits about him for what was in store.

'Right lads, let's make a move.' Just over fifty ICF lads made for the exit. The pub owner looked thoroughly bemused as his pub rapidly emptied just as quickly as it had filled up. Some folk were leaving near full pints behind. Mind you, not many empty glasses or bottles were left on the tables.

ICF were on their way.

CHAPTER THIRTY
ICF v ASC

The street was near some sort of run-down industrial estate and was deserted at this time on a Saturday night. If everyone could make it there undetected then the setting was absolutely perfect for what was about to happen.

There was no visible CCTV. There were no police and no nosey neighbours to film anything for fucking Facebook.

The plan which had been agreed between both mobs in advance was for Rangers to come from the bottom end of the street and Aberdeen to come from the top end and then it was in the lap of the God's.

The police wouldn't be on the lookout for mobs in Glasgow, especially in this location. Rangers weren't playing until Sunday. Celtic's game had been moved to Monday night. Thistle had played earlier but against Stenhousemuir, so there'd be no prospect of trouble and the game wouldn't be on the old bills radar. Plus, Aberdeen's mob hadn't gone anywhere near the game against Queens Park. There would probably be a few NGE with Aberdeen, although the Thistle lads Davie knew hadn't mentioned it.

Rangers had made it to the arranged meet with no problems whatsoever. Hopefully, the ASC would follow suit. Everyone was bouncing on their toes and waiting eagerly for it to go right off. They were all trying to be as quiet as possible, so no one was alerted to what was going on, but it was hard work trying to keep a lid on fifty excited and adrenaline fuelled lads.

A minute or two passed, it felt longer. Much longer.

'Fucking sheep have shat it.' one of the younger ones said.

'Keep it together.'

You could cut the tension with a knife.

'Go and see if you can see them- '

However, just at that a noise sounded and up ahead around forty odd Aberdeen lads came into view. Davie knew the ASC would never have shat it in a month of Sunday's. Aberdeen might be a lot of things, but they weren't shitebags. There was no way they'd be a no show, not after going to all the trouble of meeting McKee and sorting the venue like that. They'd never live it down if they didn't turn up.

Both sides moved towards each other. Here we fuckin go, Davie thought. One of the younger ones actually shouted it.

'Here we fuckin go!'

'No cunt better run. C'mon Rangers let's fuckin do this!' There was zero chance of anyone running, apart from right into each other.

'ICF! ICF!'

'Fuckin stand Aberdeen. Into these weegie cunts.'

A few bottles and pint glasses flew overhead from both sides and then a huge roar went up. Both mobs were running full steam ahead at each other. It was like something out of Braveheart although everyone was much better dressed for the occasion and there was no fucking face paint in sight.

If you could bottle the feeling of steaming into an opposing mob with a load of your good pals, you'd be a fucking millionaire.

Davie was near the front and met the action quickly. Mob fights like this were always messy affairs. He knew that if you went down then that was it, you'd take a kicking and be lucky to get back on your feet. He flew into Aberdeen's mob connecting with a small guy with a horrible, padded Barbour hat on. He smacked him right in the mouth and could feel a satisfying crack. Then he surged forward. He recognised a mouthy wee fucker who'd been going with Aberdeen for years. One of their top boys. He'd always had a bee in his bonnet about Rangers. Paton was forever telling him about all the shite he was writing on social media trying to wind Rangers lads up. Davie headed for him but before he made it, he received a huge smash to the side of the head from some big scruffy farmer looking cunt. The big farmer was about 6ft 8 and screamed 'Aaaiiiiberdeen' right in his face with that stupid fuckin horrible accent. Davie didn't know what the fuck was going on. He didn't know if it was New York or New Year. Everything was swimming. Fucking hell... the big farmer cunt had hands like fuckin shovels. Don't go down, don't go down, Davie told himself. This was fucking carnage. Davie just about managed to keep his feet and stumbled backwards away from more flying fists and kicks. Thankfully, the big farmer with the genetically modified hands had moved on to some other poor fucker.

Davie stopped for a second and looked around. Tried to compose himself. Tried to get his head to stop spinning. He took in the scene in front of him. This was absolutely bonkers. It was chaos. It was fucking brilliant.

A punch to the top of his head tore Davie sharply from his daydream. Thankfully, it wasn't a good dig. If it'd been from the big farmer, then it would have been goodnight Vienna. The punch had come from a wee daft looking younger Aberdeen.

'Mon then ya sheep cunt!'

The glancing punch had done Davie a favour, his head had just about cleared. He was in the middle of the action once again. Straight away Davie got another whack across the head from some ASC nutter with no front teeth. What the fuck was going on here? How come he was getting targeted by all these nutters. He was taking a fuckin pasting. This must be how Second prize Paton felt all the time. This couldn't be allowed to stand, after all the build-up and preparation there was no way he was going to remember it for all the wrong reasons. He gathered himself together again and launched into the psycho looking cunt, he connected with a decent punch to the guy's nose. Before he knew it, he had been pushed along into another battle. At least he was holding his own now.

Both sides were going toe to toe, not one inch was being given or taken. Neither side seemed to be on top, although it was hard to tell from the middle of a row how it was going. No side was legging the other in any case. Davie had at least managed to get the upper hand for once during the action.

A few bodies were strewn on the ground, two lads looked as if they were out cold, Davie thought it was one from each side, but he couldn't be sure with all the carnage happening around him. A few lads on both sides had taken backwards steps to either nurse their wounds or regroup. Fair fuck's to boxers going twelve three minute rounds, the row had only been going on for a few minutes and Davie was already knackered. He wasn't the only one.

Unfortunately, two police had arrived on the scene, they must have stumbled across this mess and wondered what the fuck was going on. Or someone had seen what was going on from their business premises and wondered what the fuck was happening at this time on a normally quiet Saturday night. The old bill were trying, unsuccessfully, to stop the fighting. There was no chance they could arrest anyone. Not unless they wanted a kicking. They were frantically shouting for back up into their radios and both had their extendable batons drawn out but didn't look up for using them. However, the presence of the old bill and the fact they were screaming for backup and telling anyone who'd listen that they were filming the incident with body cameras was enough for some of the lads on both sides and the groups were starting to slowly disperse. Davie was glad in one way, he was absolutely fucking done in, and he didn't fancy getting nicked for this. There would be a few heavy sentences dished out if anyone was caught for an organised meet when their team wasn't even playing. The fighting had been going on for a couple of minutes, but it had seemed like forever. Davie certainly wasn't as fit as he used to be, plus his head was spinning again. Another couple of police officers had arrived at the top of the street and this led to most lads moving off sharpish and calling it a day before any arrests were made. Davie grabbed Andy who was bleeding from a small head cut (surprise, surprise) and they headed off before more old bill arrived on the scene. Hopefully, everyone would make it away.

What a fuckin buzz.

CHAPTER THIRTY-ONE
Pub stories

More ICF lads than usual were in the pub the Saturday after the Aberdeen fight. This normally happened after a big event. Everyone wanted to talk about what had gone on.

In Davie's mind, neither mob could claim a clear result from the off. Both sides had gone at it hammer and tongs, no one had budged an inch and there were injuries on both sides. Fair play to both mobs. Davie didn't like to admit it, but he was more than impressed with the ASC. It took a lot of bottle travelling all that way and following instructions from an opposing mob which led them into an industrial estate. Davie may not like the ASC or anyone from Aberdeen for that matter, but credit where it was due. Loads of mob's bottle would have well and truly crashed. He'd heard Aberdeen had been set up in the Ukraine when they played Dnipro years ago, they'd been led into a dodgy housing estate and been well outnumbered, a few had taken sore ones, so fair fucks to them for partaking this time when it could have easily happened again. In the pub, most ICF were trying to claim a result, no doubt in Aberdeen the ASC were doing likewise. Davie knew that a few messages had been exchanged between the two mobs giving grudging respect to each other and both firms would look forward to doing it all over again. Although the chances of that ever happening were slim as the police would be on top of both mobs for a good while to come.

Andy Paton, or Second Prize Paton, arrived at the pub to a roar of laughter and back slapping. He had two black eyes and a stupid big plaster on his forehead. He really was a wee jinxed bastard and more and more lads had started using the Second Prize nickname. He couldn't expect anything else. To be fair to him, he took it all in good spirits.

'Fucking hell Andy, didn't think it was that bad.' Davie said.

'Some big farmer went to town on me man, his hands were like big fuckin spades...'

Davie tried not to laugh too much. Second Prize Paton strikes again. Davie knew exactly who had gone to town on Andy, it was the same near seven-foot chookter who had smashed him on the side of the head.

'Thank fuck Clemmy rescued me when he did, the big farmer could've killed me.' Paton said.

'Aye, he was a big boy right enough, we had a good toe to toe.' Clemmy said. 'It took me to sort him out, ain't that right Wilson?' Clemmy was smiling at Davie, he must've witnessed what had happened to him.

'Aye, very good. It was some dig he caught me with. Thought my head was gonna fly off my shoulders.' Davie said.

'And then the big fucker turned his attention to wee Second Prize Paton!' Billy McKay was almost doubled over laughing.

'Aye, I'm always sorting out Wilson's problems for him.' Paton laughed.

'Fair play to ye, ya wee prick.' McKay slapped Paton on the back. High praise indeed coming from McKay.

There were meat wagons outside the pub and coppers stationed at the entrance even though they knew the threat of violence was non-existent, it was a complete waste of taxpayers' money but an easy shift for them all the same. The old bill knew they'd missed all the fun last week, they knew they'd been caught on the hop and didn't like it one little bit. Happy Gilmour was

140

taking pelters as usual and had lost his temper, threatening a few lads with arrest. Davie wondered how things were at home with his wife these days, wondered if he was still in the bad books after what had happened at the restaurant. There was even a wee young copper who looked as if he was on work experience filming everyone who entered and left the pub. What a job these guys had, sitting in a police van doing absolutely fuck all and probably getting paid double time for the privilege. The polis knew they had nothing to go on with the Aberdeen fight and knew they couldn't make anything stick, nothing that would hold up in court anyway. The only way they'd find out more about the off was if lads from either mob grassed and that was never going to happen.

The pub was full of stories from everyone's viewpoints of the row with the ASC. Lads who hadn't done much at all in Davie's mind were claiming this and that and no one was going to disagree. As the years went on the stories would grow arms and legs and some lads would claim they did all sorts. That was the thing about big offs like that, no one was keeping tabs on the whole thing and seeing who was doing what. Everyone remembered things differently. Davie for his part, could remember a few of his friend's getting tore in but he hadn't seen what half of them had got up to. He had his own problems during the fight and had, after a fairly ropey start, managed to hold his own. It was a good buzz hearing about different things which had taken place. There was always lots of goings on that you didn't know about. Davie also found it funny to hear some lads talking about seeing what had happened to him during the row.

'How is wee Grant McPhee?' Clemmy said. McPhee was part of the younger lot and at the same school as Davie's son.

'How what happened to him?' Davie said.

141

'He was ko'd early doors, took a good dig from some chookter and it was goodnight from him. Sparked right out.' Clemmy said. Davie looked around the pub but the two young one's from his son's school didn't seem to be there.

'He's still a bit fucked.' Paton said, 'I talked to him during the week, doctors said he had a bad concussion and his eyes fucked. Think he might need an operation on it. He said coppers turned up at his bedside at the hospital, but he told them he'd no idea what had happened or how he'd ended up there. To be fair, he's probably telling the truth because he really doesn't remember anything about the day. He didn't know anything about any row with Aberdeen.'

'As long as he kept his mouth shut.' McKee said. He really was all heart, but he was also one hundred per cent right, if young guys wanted to go running with the mob, then when it came on top or the police had you in for interview then it was 'no comment' all the way. Only thing worse than a runner was a fuckin grass. He hoped the wee man was alright though, concussion and a possible operation on his eye didn't sound good at all.

Happy Gilmour was trying to find out more information about what had happened and was trying to get lads on their own to ask his stupid questions. Only an utter mug would have told him anything. He'd grabbed Andy aside and asked him how he'd got the black eyes. Andy just laughed and told him he was being beaten up by his missus which had gone down like a lead balloon.

However, as the weeks went on, it was back to a severe lack of action and numbers were dwindling again. Nowadays, most of the older lot had stopped going all the time, they had families, businesses, or both. Not many folk were eager to get nicked for a small dash at the football. Football and football violence were no longer a priority. Davie could understand it, but he couldn't help himself being out most weeks. What if he missed something? There were always a few older lads out, so it wasn't like it was just him and the youth. That would have been a bit weird. Although, even if it was just him and the youth, Davie didn't like to admit it, but he would probably still go. He loved reminiscing about the good old days even though everyone had heard the old war stories numerous times. For a spell he had taken Allan to some games, but he wasn't showing much interest in going to Ibrox and that suited Davie down to the ground. Now it turned out he was hanging about with boys from Allan's school.

Rangers and Celtic were battling it out to win the league and they were still in the Scottish cup. The draw for the quarter finals was being made later that night which, rather sadly, would be the highlight of Davie's weekend. Remarkably Airdrie who were in League One and were utter dogshit still hadn't been papped out yet, so there was a chance of a meeting with them. Motherwell who were a decent mob, especially in the cup, were another good option. Partick Thistle had also somehow made it to the quarters as well and they were a decent mob but not one Davie was looking for in the draw. Celtic were also still in it, so there were four decent ties which could be drawn. For a change, there were lots of potential offs in the draw. Motherwell and Airdrie would be decent. Airdrie and Thistle was always lively. Davie was hoping Rangers would be drawn against either Celtic or Airdrie. If it was Celtic, then hopefully this time he wouldn't miss all the action and if it was Airdrie then it was time for some payback after what they'd done to him at Hamilton.

The Scottish Cup draw wasn't even on the telly, fucking YouTube had it streaming live. Scottish football really was a mess. The draw used to be a big thing and now it wasn't even on television. Half the time the powers that be couldn't even get a sponsor for their flagship competition and had sold TV rights to tinpot companies for buttons. Bear in mind this was the same people who had thought it a good idea to demote Rangers through the leagues costing themselves an absolute fortune, what was the phrase? Turkeys voting for Christmas.

Paton was watching the draw on his phone but no one else seemed to be remotely interested. Young Second Prize was getting frustrated as either his phone or the poxy stream was buffering. After what seemed like an age, Andy looked somewhat excited.

'Airdrie away!' Paton shouted over.

The tie Davie wanted.

'Ya fuckin dancer.' Davie said to himself. He certainly had a score to settle with them after the Hamilton farce. Although, in fairness to Airdrie, they could have been a lot worse with him. He vaguely could remember some of the Section B lads making sure he wasn't too badly hurt after all the Hamilton shitebags had fled. But still, they'd turned him over and now he had a chance to put it right. The game would get the lads out, he was sure of it. They'd came up against the Section B a few years back and it had been fun, they'd run a couple of them into the local Spar shop. This had led to much slagging from many mobs which Airdrie were none too happy about. So maybe they'd be looking for a bit of revenge. Then a few Rangers had been nicked after an off with Wigan who had plenty of Airdrie with them. Wigan would surely be up for this one. So, all in all, there was a right good chance of both mobs being up for it. Plus, it was the Scottish cup and something a bit different. It was time to inject a bit of life back into Scotland's premier cup competition.

CHAPTER THIRTY-TWO
Chased by a woman with no teeth

Davie was out for his lunch on Sauchiehall Street, not too far from the office when he spotted her. There was no mistaking her. It was NaeTeeth. Fully clad in her Celtic home kit again, she even had the shorts and socks on. The number 67 and 'The Big One' written on her back. He quickly dived into the nearest shop for fear of being seen. She was looking up and down the street for something or someone. He'd sent her an email the previous day trying to let her down gently and had received a barrage of misspelled abuse in reply. She'd told him in no uncertain terms that she needed him to sort out her father's house. She wasn't taking no for an answer. He wasn't even sure if he was to try and re-mortgage the place or sell it anymore.

She couldn't be looking for him, surely not. Davie stood watching her from the shop which he had entered.

'Can I help you sir?' the security guard stationed at the entrance said.

'Eh, no mate, I'm just having a wee look around.' Davie turned and saw the bulky security guard look at him as if he had two heads. On looking further into the shop, Davie could see why. There were female mannequins with all sorts of lingerie on. He'd fucking jumped into Ann Summers.

The security guard was still glaring at him.

'Listen mate, I'm just trying to avoid someone,' Davie started then stopped, why the fuck was he justifying himself to this jobsworth prick?

Davie watched as NaeTeeth turned and started heading in the direction of his office. There was something odd about the way she walked. It was her trainers. They looked far too big for her. She had big clown feet- wait a fucking minute. Davie recognised the trainers, he should do, he had paid eighty fuckin quid for them. The little tramp was wearing his trainers. The little no toothed cow had stolen his packages. Davie stared the security guard down and left Ann Summers trying to act as if he had the moral high ground. He walked out standing tall and started to follow NaeTeeth, who unfortunately by this time seemed to have figured out where his office was. It all fell into place in Davie's mind. How had he not put two and two together. Of course she'd figured out where his office was, she'd been before and helped herself to his new trainers and a nice, not to mention expensive, top. At least there was a buzzer entry to the office, and she wouldn't be able to get- Aw fuck, some Just Eat delivery guy was leaving the building and held the door open for her. How fucking lucky was that. Davie knew he couldn't go back to the office now, not without facing her.

Davie had waited outside for nearly an hour now and still she hadn't exited the building. This was ridiculous, she wasn't going to give up and he needed to get back in. He had lined up all sorts of calls for this afternoon and couldn't afford to miss them. Plus, he really needed to go to the toilet. A thought struck him, he could climb up the fire escape around the back - Naeteeth wouldn't even know he was in the office as she'd be waiting outside his locked door. If he climbed up the fire escape, then he'd avoid having to deal with her.

He was starting to make his way around the back of the premises to the fire escape when the door to the building opened and Naeteeth appeared.

'There you are!' she said.

'Listen, you need to stop this.' Enough was enough, Davie needed to tell her in no uncertain terms that he couldn't deal with her. This was embarrassing. He was going to climb up the fire escape just to avoid her for fuck's sake. 'I've told you in my email and now I'll tell you to your face. I can't get you or your dad a deal on the house. I can't work with you.'

'How no?'

Davie didn't have an answer ready, he stuttered and then came out with it.

'I think you're taking advantage of your father, and I don't want any part of it. So stop phoning me, stop messaging me, stop coming to my office and stop thieving my fucking trainers!'

Naeteeth looked mad.

'What? Your one mad bastard telling me no…'

Suddenly Naeteeth swung a punch at Davie who moved back out of reach. She started swinging left's and rights wildly. Fucking hell, this had escalated quickly. Davie thought about giving her a swift dig to the chops but something stopped him. She may not look like it, but she was a woman after all and he didn't hit women, even though she was trying to smash him. Plus, he knew where this would go, she'd get the police involved and play the victim, try to get money out of him someway. No, he couldn't be dealing with all that. Davie moved backwards again, out of her reach. Then she started chasing him, Davie was getting backed off by a Celtic kitted woman with no gnashers. Worse than backed off, he was getting legged up Sauchiehall Street.

'Come here you fuckin prick, stringing me along like that, it's no on!' she shouted, shoppers turned to stare at the scene unfolding in front of them. She was making it sound as if they had been in some sort of relationship.

Davie ran back the way he'd come, the security guard at Ann Summers looked stunned as he legged it by the store with Naeteeth chasing behind.

Davie was slowly but surely getting away from her, it didn't help that she couldn't run too fast because her trainers were nearly flying off her feet. He turned down into Holland Street and started to loop his way back to the office.

Chased up Sauchiehall Street by a bird with nae gnashers wearing a full Celtic kit and trainers which he'd bought, this was fuckin embarrassing.

CHAPTER THIRTY-THREE
Airdrie away

Television ruins many things in football these days but on this occasion Premier Sport had decided that a fuckin 5:30 kick off on a Saturday night was a good idea. Everyone was surprised the police had allowed it to be honest.

Years ago, Rangers would have easily taken 200 plus good lads to a game like this but for some reason loads seemed to either not be up for it or were calling off at the last minute. For many, Airdrie away didn't hold the appeal it did for Davie. However, Davie knew looking around him that they had enough good bodies to smash a firm like Airdrie. There must have been around 30 proper old school ICF, 20 really good younger ICF and around 25/30 young Union Bear types who were probably friends with his son. So around 75 lads. A decent firm but nothing like the Rangers of old.

The 5:30 kick off left plenty of scope for an off before, during and after the game. The plan was to get through to a place beside Airdrie called Chapelhall and then from there either call it on with the B or make their way to Airdrie and hope they could meet them on route. In Davie's experience Airdrie always came out to play, especially if they fancied their chances and today, he'd heard they would have a mob of around 100 out. Some of their pals from Wigan would no doubt be up eager to payback Rangers. Not very often would Rangers be outnumbered in a place like this, but Davie was still confident enough. It didn't matter the numbers, he'd be confident going with the 30 old school lads. In fact, that might actually be preferable as there was more chance of them avoiding old bill and having a good go at them. In and out Friday night Hamilton style.

Rangers had made it through to the pub at Chapelhall and initially things had seemed promising. A few phone calls had been made and Airdrie said they would meet Rangers, told them to make their way to Airdrie and they'd find them. That was when things started to go pear shaped. Everyone gathered together to leave the pub just as a meat wagon pulled up outside. Rangers tried to move off quickly, but they'd hardly begun their journey when the cavalry turned up. Police cars, vans and then eventually a couple of horses. It wouldn't be a surprise if the policing budget had stretched to a fucking helicopter. The fun was over before it had even begun. Then to top things off it had started to rain and not just a little drizzle, it was fucking teeming it down.

'We're going to split you up into two groups,' the main copper started to shout. 'First group is those of you with match tickets. I want you all over here to the left. Those without match tickets I want over to the right.'

Most of the Rangers mob had tickets as they'd thought there was more chance of trouble around the stadium. The Shyberry Excelsior or Penny Chews Stadium or whatever the fuck it was called this week. There were only a handful of ICF who didn't have match tickets. Scott McKee was part of that group along with John McDonald. McKee looked furious as they'd just been told they were going to get escorted straight to the train station where they'd be put on the first train heading back to Glasgow, even though they'd come by bus. The Old Bill weren't for listening. Whatever happened to a person's human rights? In fairness, Davie thought that didn't sound like the worst idea in the world, as there was no way they'd see any action now, not with half of Police Scotland watching over them. Plus, the rain was that heavy it had soaked through to Davie's underwear.

Airdrie were going by in cars looking at the escort as the main mob were taken to the game. Davie was sure he'd spotted the big

150

scruffy cunt from his Hamilton kicking but to be fair there were a good few Airdrie who looked and dressed like that. Some of them looked as if they were permanently stuck in the eighties with their skinheads and Doc Martens. Airdrie was a strange backwards place.

Davie and the rest of them could see the Section B at the game, you couldn't fucking well miss them as they were beside a big stupid red flag with a fucking picture of Donald Trump on it which said 'Making Airdrie Great Again'. You couldn't make this shit up. There looked to be about 50 or so of them.

During the game, the police were picking off any ICF who had the audacity to go to the toilet. They were getting searched, presumably for Class A's. Clemmy never came back from going for a line and a few had said they'd seen him getting a pull. Hopefully, he didn't have much on him.

A few ICF had tried to leave the game just after half time, but the Old Bill had been wise to that one as well and nipped that in the bud. Again, the big bad casuals of the world had no rights and couldn't even leave a football match early. The whole day was turning into a complete fucking disaster.

Soaking wet and wrapped up by old bill, could today get any worse. Only Clemmy was having a worse day. After the game, Rangers were surrounded by police as they headed back to the buses and trains and that's when they saw Airdrie again. Airdrie's numbers had swelled to around 70 or 80 lads, which in this day and age is very decent. If only the ICF could have got near them.

Davie and his group of ICF tried to hold back and get out the back of the escort but by this point there were a few police horses, and it was impossible to get through. Airdrie were making a half-hearted attempt to get at Rangers but again the police were the only ones winning the day. Plus, if it had kicked off, the old bill knew just about everyone who was there and most of them were wearing body cameras filming everything that went on, so doors would undoubtedly be going in.

Soaked to the skin and surrounded by tons of police, this wasn't how it was meant to go.

'Time to give all this shit up Davie.' Happy Gilmour said to him, trying to be all pally. He said it as if he was an old friend passing on some sage advice. He hated it when the Football Intelligence used his name, especially this particular Football Intelligence Officer.

Aye, you're probably right, Davie thought but he wasn't going to give the big lanky cunt the satisfaction of an answer. He just stared at the copper with a look of disgust. Thought about asking him how things were at home with the wife. Ask him if he'd been playing away again with someone from work.

The lanky streak of piss FI old bill was probably right, but Davie Wilson wasn't ready to give it up...

He was still enjoying himself far too much.

Printed in Great Britain
by Amazon

11807753R10092